The

Comforts

The Comforts

BLAKE CHANNELS

Blossom Cove Publishing

For my beautiful daughters –
Dream big and believe in yourselves. You will go far.

CHAPTER 1

February 2115

Island of Inizi

TALIA DELANEY SAT in her tiny room within the palace walls, wringing her hands in dreaded anticipation. The autumn season whispered in the distance, an affirmation that Talia was of age and would soon take her place as one of the Comforts. Some of the girls she'd come to know over the years were looking forward to this day. They romanticized the thought of giving themselves over to a noble and perhaps becoming a lifelong mate to one.

Talia did not feel the same. Assisting her mother as an aid in the hospital prior to being selected as a Comfort, Talia had witnessed her fill of shattered young women admitted after fulfilling their *duties* as a

Comfort. In addition to nursing cuts and bruises, she and her mother had consoled the broken hearts of those who had dared to dream of the finer things their life as a Comfort might bring. Talia recalled her mother's soothing voice and strong, but elegant hands, and felt a pang of sadness.

There was a soft knock on the door and a tall, slender woman with graying brown hair entered the room, clutching a blue gown to her bosom. Her hair was pulled back in a neat bun and Talia surmised that at one time the woman was probably quite pretty. Her oval-shaped face boasted high cheekbones and a small, upturned nose with a smattering of freckles. But despite the woman's delicate features, her face was etched in hard lines and she had an air of sadness about her. The woman greeted Talia with a tight smile, but her eyes were sympathetic.

"My name's Rebecca. I've been tasked with getting you ready for this evening."

Talia nodded, but didn't introduce herself, presuming that if Rebecca was assigned to her, she was most certainly aware of her name. She studied the woman instead. Rebecca wore a green, sleeveless dress and Talia couldn't help but notice the small tattoo on the woman's shoulder blade when she turned to close the door behind her. It was faded, but Talia could still make out the intricate design.

"You must be a seasoned Comfort," Talia said, unsure if her spoken observation was impolite.

"I was," Rebecca said, straightening her shoulders and holding her head high. "Now I am a handmaid for King Lachlan."

Talia did her best not to shudder.

King Lachlan was the fourth-generation ruler of the island of Inizi. Italian for *beginnings*, Inizi was once known as Tasmania, but seceded from

Australia during the Great World War of 2047 when it became its own nation – a nation that would serve under the rule of a European king. The first king of Inizi erected an extravagant palace and established a monarchy in which the middle class was all but dissolved. The upper-class citizens were permitted to live within the great walls of the kingdom, while the poor were forced to dwell in cramped, rundown housing in townships outside the palace walls.

Although the island's first king valued technology and much of the luxuries the modern age offered, he had a peculiar obsession with Europe's Medieval Era. He loved the architecture, the elaborate clothing, but most of all, he loved the antiquated culture; a culture that accepted a monarchial rule and didn't overtly question disparity or an overreaching regime. The first king forced his obsession on the inhabitants of the island – imposing dress codes, property covenants, and laws of conduct that mirrored much of the old-fashioned customs from the Middle Ages, while still embracing new-age amenities. These ideals were passed from generation to generation and remained an unchallenged way of life for the people of Inizi.

Contrary to its name, to Talia, the island of *beginnings* now represented the bitter expiry of her childhood. Each year, fifteen young girls of sixteen years of age were selected from the poorer townships. For some families, this was considered a great honor; likened to winning a social lottery. The parents were paid handsomely to turn their daughters over to the palace, and the young girls were well-provided for.

Each girl was imprinted with a small tattoo on her right shoulder blade, baring the king's family crest – the letter "L," boldly stenciled in red, symbolizing the Lachlan family name. The "L" was framed by silver-tipped angel wings and overlaid by twin, crisscrossed swords with *regno di forza* (kingdom of strength) inscribed on each rounded sword handle. The tattoo was said to be a mark of esteem, but in actuality it deterred the girls from running away. The emblem was distinct and easy to recognize. The girls were pampered and refined until the age of eighteen. Then, finally of an appropriate age by society's standards, they were considered *in season*, and ready to fulfill their obligations to a nobleman.

An annual celebration, the Harvest Ball (a name in poor taste, in Talia's mind), was held to introduce the new *crop* of Comforts to society. There was music, dancing, food, and, for the highlight of the evening – an auction. Each young woman was dressed in the finest clothes and put on display to be selected amongst society's noblemen. At the celebration, the single men were the only ones allowed to bid for a virgin Comfort. The money raised during the celebration was donated to charity, cleansing society's conscience of the fact they were offering young women into sexual bondage. The *privileged* young woman was then whisked away to spend her evening as the noble desired.

Once a Comfort fulfilled her first night with a lord, she was considered a *seasoned* Comfort. While still well-provided for, her life was no longer as luxurious. She was housed with the other seasoned Comforts and could be beckoned by any nobleman, including the married men. Especially the married men. After a seasoned Comfort reached the age of thirty, she could seek employment amongst the society members. If unable to gain employment, she was cast out completely – left to fend for herself outside the palace walls.

Realizing that she had been staring, Talia looked down at the floor and wondered how many lords Rebecca had endured throughout her years as a Comfort and how long it took before Rebecca's spirit had faded, along with her beauty.

"I brought you a really pretty, cornflower blue dress," Rebecca told her. "It will match your eyes and help you get noticed."

"I don't want to get noticed," Talia said, spitting her words out through gritted teeth.

"Don't be a fool. It is your duty," Rebecca scolded, her eyes darting around the room. Talia's stomach twisted in knots as she contemplated whether Rebecca believed her own statement or if she was worried someone might be listening in.

Talia crossed the room and snatched the dress from Rebecca's hands, refusing her offer of assistance. "Come out when you are dressed, and I will see what I can do with that hair," Rebecca instructed before making her departure.

Sighing, Talia sunk onto the bed, trying to gather her wits and willing herself not to cry. She should be ready for this day; she'd been preparing for it for two years. That is, her tutors had prepped her for this day. But now that it was here, she was more afraid than ever. Despite her efforts, she felt a tear escape and roll down her cheek. Wiping it away in anger, she stood, squared her shoulders, and began to get dressed, determined not to show weakness.

Moments later Talia appeared serene as she stepped out of her bedroom. She made her way to the powder room where Rebecca was waiting for her, hairbrush in hand. She forced a smile as she took a seat on the round, cushioned stool in front of the silver vanity.

5

With nimble fingers, Rebecca combed and curled Talia's hair. Talia sat in silence, appearing stoic and graceful – though she identified with neither.

Kaden Huff appeared soon after. He sneered as he struck the doorframe with his handsome cane, startling both women. Tall and muscular, with chiseled looks, those who didn't know him were blinded by appearances and mistook him to be charming. Talia despised him. Although he came from a wealthy family, Kaden squandered his inheritance by over-indulging his playboy lifestyle. Women. Gambling. Whatever fancied him. After settling his debts, he was forced to work to keep his place in society and to maintain the lavish lifestyle he was accustomed to. By night he trolled the palace parties and rubbed elbows with society's finest – keeping up appearances of his assumed wealth. By day, he was tasked with looking after the well-being of the virgin Comforts and was given strict instructions not to harm or defile any of them.

Although Kaden was smart enough not to deflower any of the girls, he tormented and punished them. He was clever at hurting them in ways that didn't leave a mark. Talia had more than once fallen victim to his brutality, and she seethed from her seat, doing her best to avoid eye contact.

"Hello there, my little flower," he said, his words laced in cruelty. Talia hated the nickname she had been subjected to since the tender age of sixteen. Her first instinct was to cower, but instead she stared coolly up at him, matching his frosty gaze.

"You have no business here," Rebecca scolded him, and Talia was surprised at the woman's bravery. "I have a duty to get her ready for tonight's celebration and you will only be in the way here," she said, shooing him out with the hairbrush.

Kaden's expression turned murderous, but he tipped his hat, bowed, and exited the room. Talia exhaled slowly, relieved he was gone. "Let us hope that he doesn't try to bid on you," Rebecca muttered, returning her attention to Talia's hair.

Talia felt a surge of nausea and panic. She'd spent the past two years trying to avoid his advances and felt some assurances he would never be daft enough to force himself on her. But she had never considered that he might be amongst the nobles making an offer for her.

"Oh, I'm sure there will be much prettier Comforts at the celebration for him to choose from," she managed to say, but her voice shook, and her tone lacked conviction. Rebecca gave Talia's hand a sympathetic pat and proceeded to brush out her tangled mane.

CHAPTER 2

TWO HOURS LATER, Talia was ready for her reveal. Her dark hair was piled high atop her head, with small curls cascading around her forehead and nape of her neck. Her makeup had been expertly applied and her blue dress was altered to fit snuggly at her narrow waist while still flowing behind her like a bridal train. She wore a necklace made of diamonds and teardrop sapphires – on loan from the king's personal jeweler. Silver designer shoes boasting an open toe and three-inch heel completed the ensemble.

"You look beautiful," Rebecca said, beaming with pride. Talia did her best not to lash out in anger. She didn't want to look beautiful. She wanted to go unnoticed. With any luck, she wouldn't be selected by any of the bidders. Perhaps they would find her dull and she would be returned to her township where she could live in peace. She was certain – well, moderately certain – she could learn how to provide for herself.

After offering Rebecca a tight smile and thanking her for her efforts, though she didn't feel particularly grateful, Talia took her place in line amongst the other Comforts. Although she had spent the past two years with these girls, and knew all their names, she was only close to a few. She knew getting too attached would prove painful in the end; that it would take all she had to handle the cards she'd been dealt and the last thing she needed was to weep and fret over the plight of others.

Many of the girls were bustling with excitement and Talia felt a dull ache in the pit of her stomach. Those girls would be the most disappointed of the lot, she feared. A few of the girls were crying softly, but the rest remained silent, looking as terrified as Talia felt.

After each being fitted with a corded silver bracelet that Talia suspected was some sort of tracking device, the virgin Comforts were led down a corridor and lined up backstage in one of the great banquet halls. Through the mauve, velvet curtain the girls could hear a booming voice announce their arrival, followed by thunderous applause and a few hoots and hollers from the crowd. The bile rose up in Talia's throat and she clenched her fists at her sides, desperately trying to wield her courage. Carly, the tall, lanky girl in front of her, burst into tears and Talia reached up to pat her shoulder, telling her everything would be alright, though she knew full well it probably wouldn't be.

All at once the heavy curtain opened and the Comforts were greeted with more applause and crashing symbols from the band. Talia held her head high and glared into the crowd with prideful disdain. Her mouth felt dry, and although her lips were well-glossed, she licked them in apprehension.

One by one the Comforts stepped forward, subjecting themselves to be bid upon. Blaire, a pretty, brown-haired girl in a yellow taffeta gown with eyelet lace was the first in line. She appeared pleased with the bidding and curtsied to the crowd. The bidders responded to her stage presence, and she went for a high price. The second girl in line, Madelyn, was draped in a pale-pink, chiffon dress and wore a feathered bonnet to cover the fact she was not as fair. Recruiters were trained to select the prettiest crop each year. The murmuring from the crowd and lack of bidding activity suggested that, in this instance, the recruiter may have had an off day.

There was one bid, but Madelyn was selected, and the third girl, Sephora, stepped forward. Sephora was one of the few remaining on the island who was of Aboriginal descent and the crowd gasped in response to her exotic beauty. Her cream gown complemented her dark features. With soft, brown eyes, she smiled politely into the crowd, and a small dimple fluttered on her cheek. The bidding was erratic amongst the throng of would-be suitors, but the one with the deepest pockets eventually won out.

Throughout the frenzied bidding, and even while she was being led off stage, Sephora remained serene, her shoulders squared. For a moment, Talia forgot her surroundings and stood in awe of Sephora's demonstration of unruffled composure. But when the next girl stepped to the front of the stage, and the line of Comforts shifted forward, Talia was yanked back to reality.

Talia was seventh in line, and with each bid her heart beat more wildly in her chest. She fiddled with the pretty sapphire necklace, finding small solace in the smoothness of the stones against her fingertips. When it was her turn to step forward, she was dazed by the bright spotlight. She tripped over her own feet and nearly toppled off the stage. The crowd roared with laughter. Talia was furious. She picked up a tall urn perched next to her on the stage and lifted it high as if to throw it into the crowd.

"That's enough!" a booming voice said from across the room, startling Talia and rendering the crowd silent. "Bring that one up to my room."

The spectators murmured in hushed tones. A man in a royal blue guard's uniform with brass buttons and a red-and-gold collar appeared next to Talia, taking her by the arm and leading her off the stage. "What's going on?" she asked, confused why someone would be allowed to bypass the bidding and wondering how much trouble she was in for losing her temper.

"You didn't see who chose you?" The guard looked perplexed.

Chose? As if I'm supposed to be honored. The defiant thought surfaced just above the fear and confusion that fired in her brain. "No. Who was it?"

"That was the king's son," the guard responded, and it was everything Talia could do not to run.

Talia didn't know much about the prince. From what she'd heard, he kept mostly to himself and rarely engaged with the rest of society. He attended college abroad in the Grand Americas but returned to Inizi after graduation to be near his family and commence his royal responsibilities.

His father, King Lachlan, was another matter. Talia shuddered as she recalled the stories she'd heard about him. The king ruled harshly and was known to have taken several Comforts for himself. She could only hope the king's son was not as vile.

The guard led Talia through several corridors. Her heart and feet felt heavy, and she tread slowly across the polished marble floors. Comforts were secluded from much of society, and over the past two years she had yearned for a chance to explore the castle without boundaries. But today she was in no mood to appreciate its beauty.

In her hopelessness, she failed to notice the breathtaking limestone walls, the spiral staircases that led to private wings, or the lush greenery thrusting through the floors and cascading over doorcases. Instead she concentrated on her breathing and tried to picture her life from this point forward. She struggled to heed her mother's words of wisdom, encouraging her to find the positive in any situation. But nothing positive came to mind, and Talia's eyes stung with the reality of it all.

"This is it," the guard announced when they arrived at a massive, wooden door with hand-carved arches.

"What do I do?" she asked, feeling lost as she stood outside the vast doorway.

The guard snickered as if privy to some private joke that he'd forgotten to let Talia in on. "I'm sure the prince will let you know," he sneered. And with that, he walked away to join a second guard who sat further down the hallway, keeping a watchful eye on the prince's room.

CHAPTER 3

TALIA SUMMONED ALL her courage before knocking on the door. Her hand trembled as she returned it to her side and waited for the door to be opened to her. Although she thought she had a pretty good idea, she wasn't certain what to expect. No matter what society called it, or how accepted and entrenched in the culture it had become, she felt strongly that it was rape – plain and simple. Her stomach twisted in revulsion and dread.

The door opened, and Talia gazed upwards at the man who towered before her. The emotions that washed over her at first seeing him were a combination of terror and fascination. She supposed that he must be the prince, although he wasn't dressed like royalty. Instead he stood before her wearing a faded blue, cotton-blend shirt with tan trousers and bare feet. His hair was disheveled, evidence of a quick clothing change moments prior.

"Come in," he commanded.

Talia pushed past him, trying to appear brave. She took a seat in the posh, wingback chair in the far corner of the room, not waiting for permission. She glanced at the bed and tried not to regard it with disdain.

"What's your name?" he asked.

Not responding, for fear she would burst into tears if she opened her mouth, Talia stared down at her manicured nails as if suddenly fascinated by the shimmering pink polish. The prince walked over to her and took a seat next to her. He was handsome, more handsome than any man Talia had ever seen. His hair was dark, almost black, and his deep-set eyes were a cerulean blue. His square jawline and broad shoulders made him appear massive, even in a seated position, and Talia felt herself tremble.

"I am not going to hurt you," he said.

"Sir, I…" she started, wanting with everything within her to believe him, but she knew what was expected of her.

"Please, call me Bryce." Talia studied the prince's handsome face. The name suited him.

"I'm Talia." Her voice shook.

"Listen, Talia. I'm not going to make you do anything that you don't want to do, okay?"

Relief surged through her. The dread she'd been feeling was sliced through with a sliver of hope. She gazed shyly up at him, her eyes questioning his motives.

"I brought you up here because I thought it looked like you needed a little help back there," he explained.

She blushed, reflecting on how clumsy she must have looked nearly toppling off the stage minutes earlier. She'd blame the high heels; but then again, she'd never been very agile.

"Besides," the prince continued, "I need my father off my back. Ever since I came back he has been grilling me on why I don't have a girlfriend and why I don't take a Comfort. I thought that…" his voice trailed off.

"Oh, it must be so rough being you." The words were out of Talia's mouth before she had a chance to rein them back in. She clasped a hand over her mouth in embarrassment.

Bryce chuckled. "You really are a fiery one, aren't you?" He was unable to hide his amusement.

Talia felt relief wash over her once more. She knew she should tread lightly. Insubordination against royalty was grounds for severe punishment, or worse. "I'm sorry," she said, "sometimes I don't seem to have a filter."

"I appreciate that," he said, still chuckling. "But be careful. Others around here might not value that trait like I do."

She flashed a timid smile. "So, you're really not going to make me…"

"I find this whole thing repulsive," he interrupted.

"Well excuse me if I'm not up to your standards." Talia was surprised by her anger, but not as surprised as Bryce.

"What? Not you!" he clarified. "You, Talia, are quite beautiful. I was referring to this whole celebration and the idea that some women are someone else's property just because they are less fortunate."

Talia wasn't sure whether to feel apologetic or stunned. "So, you've never taken a Comfort?"

"Never. I prefer that my partners be willing."

She offered a tight smile, an attempt to mask the mixed emotions his comment invoked in her. On one hand, she was comforted by Bryce's admission. On the other hand, she felt an unfamiliar twinge of jealousy at his choice of the word *partners* and the thought of the other women that may have shared his bed. "So, do you want me to go back to my room, or..."

"No, feel free to stay. Everyone will be expecting you to stay the night. We wouldn't want them to grow suspicious." He winked in her direction.

Talia found herself oddly happy that the prince asked her to stay. Something about him put her at ease. "So, what does one do to pass the time in here?" she asked, looking around the enormous living quarters and noting the stark contrast to her own, modest bedroom. She spotted an old-fashioned chess table in the corner and headed towards it. "I haven't seen an actual chess set in years. And I've never seen one this fancy." She picked up one of the intricately carved marble pieces, turning it over in her hand as she studied it. "You play?"

"Well, with myself," Bryce answered, and Talia smirked rather unladylike despite her upbringing.

"I'm sorry, that came out wrong," he laughed, clearing his throat. "I mean, I can't find anyone willing to play chess with me, so I am often my only opponent."

"I love chess," she said breathily, returning the chess piece to its original position.

"Really?" He was impressed.

"Oh, yes. My dad taught me years ago and we used to play every night using wooden pieces he carved himself." Her graceful fingers straightened each piece as she spoke.

"What happened to your dad?" he asked. She stiffened. "I'm sorry, that's none of my bus…"

"He died." Her voice softened. "Both of my parents did. House fire. I was staying at a friend's house. Neither of them made it out." She grew silent, momentarily reflecting on the hole their passing had left in her heart and the devastating emptiness she still felt.

"I'm so sorry Talia." Bryce felt an overwhelming need to comfort her.

"It's okay," she said, trying not to sound so forlorn. "It was a while ago. I stayed with another family for a few months. But then when I turned sixteen…" Her voice trailed off and her delicate shoulders drooped.

The prince felt himself grow angry. "They gave you away?"

"It's not their fault," Talia defended, her voice rising. "Your father offers a great deal of money, and they had five other mouths to feed."

He knew he shouldn't judge. Bryce understood nothing about growing up in poverty. But after a few moments with Talia he was certain that, if she were under his charge, he wouldn't give her away for any sum of money.

He peered down to where she sat at the chess table. He tried not to notice the way the teardrop sapphires of her necklace grazed her plump breasts. A dark strand of hair escaped from her elegant hairclip and she tucked it behind her ear. Talia glanced up at him with her bright blue, almond-shaped eyes, then quickly looked away, embarrassed by his gaze.

"Aren't we going to play?" she asked, wiping away imaginary dust from the chess table to avoid his stare.

Realizing that he had been gawking, Bryce turned his attention to the chess board. He pulled back a chair and took a seat across from her. "Okay. But I'll warn you, I'm pretty good."

"We'll see."

CHAPTER 4

AFTER THREE MATCHES in which she bested him each time, Bryce conceded that Talia was indeed a skilled player. "It's getting late," he told her, standing to his feet and stretching his legs. "We should go to bed."

Talia stiffened. "Relax, I promise that I won't touch you. Unless of course, you want me to," he teased, but his tone was a little hopeful.

Gazing up at him, Talia was lost for words. Something about him intrigued her. Oddly, she found herself not wanting the evening to be over. "Well, there is only one bed," she pointed out, ignoring his last comment. "What will our sleeping arrangements be?"

Bryce walked over to the king-sized bed and used several plump pillows to form a boundary down the center. "That is an impenetrable wall for sure," Talia said, laughing nervously. Bryce grinned back at her, fighting the urge to kiss her and silently scolding himself to find some self-restraint.

He walked over to the handsome mahogany dresser and pulled out a white, cotton shirt, offering it to her. She looked confused. "Well, you can't sleep in that gown," he told her with a raised eyebrow.

Talia blushed down to her toes as she thought of undressing in front of the prince and donning only his shirt. "I'll close my eyes," he assured her, reading her expression.

Peeling off her dress, she slipped into the large shirt and scrambled into bed, marveling at the way the sleek sheets felt against her bare legs. She fluffed up the pillows around her for dramatic effect. Before she realized what was happening, Bryce stripped off his pants and shirt and started to remove his underneath clothes.

"What are you doing?" she asked, horrified and mesmerized at the same time. She had never seen a naked man before, aside from the sketches in her study materials, and she wasn't sure if she was quite prepared for it.

"I don't sleep in clothes, *ameerah*," he told her. She felt electricity course through her body at the nickname he gave her. *Ameerah,* she recognized as meaning *princess* in Arabic. Queen Mahira, Bryce's late great-grandmother, was a refugee from Jordan and had married into royalty. Because of her influence, Arabic was still taught in the school system and was part of the curriculum for the Comforts. Talia thought how she'd love to truly be Bryce's princess, but then dismissed the fantasy before giving it time to cultivate. The laws forbade nobles from marrying Comforts. The best she could hope for was for Bryce to allow her to stay on as his own personal Comfort, but even that opportunity was rare, and she knew better than to expect it.

Bryce climbed into bed, then removed his undershorts and tossed them on the floor. Talia turned crimson and was thankful that he had already turned off the lights. "Good night," she managed to say before turning on her side to face away from him.

At first, she found it hard to sleep. Something about having Bryce next to her was fascinating. Even through the barrier of pillows, she could feel the rhythm of his breathing. She was curious what it would feel like to have his muscular body pressed against hers. She imagined he would be firm and warm; and she felt something stir inside her. But despite her excitement, her eyelids grew heavy and she gave into her exhaustion.

Bryce stayed awake for much longer, watching her sleep and playing back in his head the moment he saw her for the first time, just hours earlier.

Truth being told he was making an obligatory appearance at the ceremony when he caught a glimpse of Talia on stage. She'd unknowingly bewitched him with all her dark hair, and flawless, creamy skin. At first, she looked like a delicate flower – as pretty and pure as a lily. But then he saw the anger flash in her deep blue eyes and watched with surprise and amusement as she lifted the vase into the air. She'd actually aimed to throw it at the crowd, and it would have served them right as far as he was concerned. But what struck a chord with him was the realization that she had fire. It danced in her eyes as she glared into the faces of the spectators. He couldn't bear the thought of someone crushing that spirit. He knew no matter how strong she was, eventually she would break.

"Bring that one to my room," he'd barked, and then walked away to try and figure out what he was going to do about the girl who captured his attention without effort.

Now he realized that he had never met anyone quite like her. While Talia might not have thought of it, Bryce found himself dreading the idea of handing her over the next morning. He wrestled with his conscience, wondering if he had done her a disservice. Tomorrow society would consider her a seasoned Comfort. She would be placed in housing with the others and any nobleman would have free rein to her. Anger bubbled up inside him at the thought of another man taking Talia's precious virginity. Before he finally drifted off to sleep, he told himself he would find a way to keep her safe.

CHAPTER 5

BRYCE AWOKE the next morning with Talia nestled in his arms. The pillow fortress between them was abandoned on the floor. Unable to stop himself, he kissed the top of her head and breathed in her sweet scent – an intoxicating combination of lavender and vanilla. She stirred, and with painstaking care, Bryce disentangled himself from her, knowing she'd be mortified if she awoke so close to him.

When her eyes fluttered open, she smiled over at him. Gazing into her eyes was like staring into the ocean and he couldn't help but think that it was a morning scene he could get used to. "Would you like breakfast?" he asked, pushing the thought aside. She nodded slowly, keenly aware that she was dressed only in a shirt and not wishing to get out of bed.

Bryce tapped the touchscreen wall panel by his side of the bed. When a voice sounded from the device, he ordered breakfast be brought up to the room. Talia felt a little embarrassed about having someone see her in bed with the prince, but her hunger won over. She also knew she'd have to get over the humiliation; being in bed with a strange man was going to be her *duty* for the foreseeable future. She shuddered at the thought.

"Are you cold?" he asked, fluffing up the covers around her. She responded with a noncommittal nod, not wanting to weigh him down with her troubles. He had been more kind to her than she deserved. She fidgeted with the palace-issued bracelet around her right wrist, realizing for the first time there was no clasp in which to remove it.

Breakfast was brought up promptly. Two servants entered the room, each wheeling in a cart; one cart overflowing with food and the second stocked with a variety of beverages. Talia did her best to avoid the sympathetic gaze from one of the servants. The aroma of warm pastries, fresh-baked bread, and English tea filled the room.

"Thank you," Bryce muttered, dismissing them with a wave of his hand. Talia was about to point out how abrupt he appeared, but she stopped herself. It wasn't her place, and she supposed indifferent treatment of servants was a learned way of life for him.

She ate her breakfast in silence, savoring every bite of sourdough toast with homemade blackberry jam and her hot cup of English tea, all the while dreading the thought of going back to her living quarters. But reality was settling in. Those wouldn't be her quarters any longer. She would be transported to housing with the other seasoned Comforts, where she would begin a life of sharing the bed of any high-society male who fancied her.

"Penny for your thoughts?" Bryce asked, although he suspected he already knew what she was thinking about. She was mulling over all the things he'd already contemplated the night before.

When she didn't answer, he worked quickly to devise a plan that would allow him to help her without her feeling like she was his charity case. He knew she would never accept anything that felt like a handout.

"Listen," he said, clearing his throat. "I'm going to be sticking around for a couple of weeks before I have to leave the country again on business. I wouldn't mind having someone around to keep me company."

She appeared hesitant.

"You can teach me a few more things about chess," he prodded.

A warm smile spread across Talia's generous lips. Her eyes brightened, and visible relief washed over her delicate features. "Alright if you'd like me to, I'll stay," she said. "Your chess moves really could use some work."

Bryce cancelled all obligations for the day and offered to give Talia an all-access tour of the palace and the grounds. "Um, I'm not sure if I can go with you," she said, her voice barely above a whisper.

"Why not?"

"I don't have anything to wear." She looked uncomfortable as she gestured with her hand, reminding Bryce that she was scantily clad in his shirt – not that he needed to be reminded.

Chuckling to himself, he made a call from the touchscreen device and ordered several gowns be brought up to the room. Minutes later Talia was gushing as she held up the garments she had to choose from, admiring the intricate detail of the beadwork, lace, and stitching.

"Do you have a preference?" she asked shyly, doing her best to conceal her bare legs behind the mound of dresses.

"Any of them will do," he said in a dismissive tone, his attention wrapped up in the paperwork one of the servants brought up with the dresses.

"If you don't have time to go with me, it's okay. I can keep myself company," she offered, fearing if she proved too great a burden, she would be sent away.

Bryce put down the paperwork and looked over at her. Tiny rays of sunshine streamed through the window, capturing Talia in their path. Her eyes shone like two bright sapphires and he ached to be near her. Obligations forgotten, he crossed the room towards her and held up the silver gown with the hand-stitched beadwork. It shimmered in the sunlight.

"I like this one," he said, holding her eyes with his gaze.

Talia smiled and glanced around for a place to change.

"The powder room is around the corner. You can take a shower before we leave," he said.

Unsure if the statement was an offer or an order, Talia obeyed and headed towards the bathroom. She was pleased to find a small travel bag on the counter, complete with a new toothbrush, toothpaste, and a hairbrush. She scrubbed her face and brushed her teeth before stepping out of the oversized shirt and into the walk-in shower. The moment her feet hit the marbled shower floor, a pleasant voice prompted her for a temperature preference.

"108 degrees," Talia said, surprised at the ease of which the random number popped into her head and slipped past her lips. She smiled with satisfaction at her newfound authority.

Steam rose around her and she closed her eyes to reflect on the past twenty-four hours. She knew she had been lucky. But now more than ever she was terrified of the days ahead and what sort of nobleman would be the first to take her to his bed. Fear washed over her, creeping up her spine. Before she could stop herself, she began to cry. Deep sobs racked her body, and she sank to the shower floor, the steamy water pelting down on her.

She heard Bryce knock on the door. "Talia? Talia, are you okay?"

Unable to answer him, she continued to cry. Concerned that she didn't respond, and hearing her muffled sobs, Bryce bolted through the door and into the steaming shower, fully clothed. He knelt beside her, stroking her hair to comfort her, seemingly unaware of her nudeness or his soaked clothing.

Talia leaned into him and kissed him bravely. She wanted to seduce him, certain that he would be gentler with her on her first time than any other man would be. She couldn't bear the thought of being ravaged by someone else.

Bryce looked confused, but his desire for her overtook him and he moved in to lengthen the kiss. "Shower off," he barked, extinguishing the water. He grabbed a plush, cream towel from its hook and wrapped Talia in it. Lifting her with minimal effort, he carried her to the bedroom. She didn't resist, but instead rested her head on his broad shoulder.

Back in the bedroom Talia became conscious of her own nakedness. Bryce set her on the bed and she scrambled to cover herself with a quilt. "You are so beautiful," he told her, unable to help himself.

She remained silent, thinking back to when she had fought the urge to scream at Rebecca and tell her that she had no desire to look beautiful.

How quickly that had changed. "I didn't mean to make you cry, Talia," he said. "I just thought you'd like a shower. I wasn't trying to imply…"

"No, it isn't that," she sniffed, cutting him off. "I just…" She couldn't continue. How could she tell someone who had been so kind to her that now more than ever she was afraid? It wasn't fair to saddle him with her problems. "It's been an emotional week, that's all." She managed a weak smile.

"Well, we can call off the tour. Stay in." The offer sounded tempting to Talia, and she thought it might give her the opportunity to coax Bryce into sleeping with her, but she also knew he'd gone through a great deal of effort to clear his schedule and she didn't want to disappoint him.

"No, no I want to go," she insisted. "Really, I'm fine. I was just having a girly moment."

Bryce smiled and planted a quick peck on her cheek. "Okay," he gave in. "You get dressed, dry your hair, and we'll head out." After changing into dry clothes, he left the room, allowing Talia full privacy. When he returned, he was holding a pair of women's flats. "I thought these would be more sensible than the shoes you wore last night," he explained.

"Now if only I had panties," Talia said, raising an eyebrow for dramatic effect.

Doing his best to suppress the image of Talia's exposed womanhood beneath her silver gown, Bryce cleared his throat and offered to arrange for some undergarments. "Oh, no, that's okay. I kind of like this free feeling," she tormented, shocked by her own flirtatious boldness.

"Good grief, woman," he said, shaking his head and chuckling to himself.

"We won't be needing an escort today," Bryce told the two guards stationed outside his door. The two men exchanged hesitant looks, but they didn't argue. Bryce linked an arm through Talia's and led her down the corridor.

The tour began with Bryce's favorite shops – antiques, sports memorabilia, and fresh pastries to satisfy his sweet tooth; followed by an expedition of the outdoor marketplace, which boasted everything from food vendors, garden-fresh fruits and vegetables, and handcrafted jewelry. After much prodding from Talia, Bryce purchased a hat and sunglasses from one of the merchants. He knew he looked ridiculous, but the ensemble made Talia laugh her carefree giggle, which was reason enough for him to comply with her request.

Talia was amazed by everything she saw, but nothing prepared her for the breathtaking gardens hidden within the palace walls. When the prince unlocked the gate and motioned her through, her eyes brightened, and her lips spread into a broad smile as she stood there, drinking it all in. Tiny walking paths interwove between expansive greenery and brilliant-colored florals. The aroma of cedar chips and fresh-cut grass were a welcome assault on her senses.

Taking Talia's hand casually in his, Bryce strolled down one of the pathways, still sporting his hat, but the sunglasses were tucked into his shirt pocket. "This is where my mother goes to relax. She spends hours in here pulling weeds and talking to her plants. It's therapeutic for her."

"Your mother maintains all this by herself?"

"No, but she does a great deal of the work. Every Tuesday we open it up to the locals as a community garden, and the grounds crew takes care of the rest."

Talia dropped his hand and crouched down, taking the earth in her palm and rubbing the rich soil between her fingertips. She touched the leaves of the camellias and leaned in to smell the aroma of the vibrant, Bulolo Gold rhododendrons. "I could spend all day in here," she said aloud.

"Well, we have lots more to see," Bryce said, pulling her to her feet and offering her a handkerchief to wipe the dirt from her hands. After returning the handkerchief to him, she offered him her arm and allowed him to lead her out of the garden, sneaking one last glance before Bryce closed the gates.

She was already impressed with the commercial area within the expansive walls of the kingdom – with its assortment of restaurants, clothing stores, and other retailers. But the residential area surprised her. Bryce led her through several small neighborhoods with postage stamp yards, but grand houses. These houses, Talia learned, were for the wealthy patrons who were not from royal bloodlines.

"There were five founding families in the first generation of Inizi," Bryce explained, "and members of these five families were deemed of *royal blood*." He rolled his eyes to demonstrate the absurdity of the belief. "Direct descendants of these families live in their own household suites within the castle itself."

"What happens when you run out of family suites?"

"Over the years, when space grew scarce, the castle was simply expanded," he said. "The castle has undergone construction on three additional wings over the years."

"How many acres are within these walls?"

"About 90," Bryce said. "But there's an additional 30 acres or so surrounding the palace walls if my father believes further expansion is needed." He paused, and a look of disapproval crossed his handsome face.

"We do open the gates to the outer townships several times a year," he continued, ashamed of how his family and friends hoarded their wealth behind the tall walls and shut the hardworking, lower class families out.

"Bryce, it's okay," she said. She didn't need him to explain. She knew his beliefs differed from his father's and his ancestors. "This is amazing," she said, stealing a glance at him. "You're amazing." This made Bryce smile and he once again took her hand in his.

As the pair continued to walk through the neighborhoods, they heard a set of windchimes tolling in the distance. "Haven't those been outlawed?" Talia groaned.

Bryce leaned in and whispered in her ear. "Do you want them to be?" His lips grazed her skin and her body shuddered with desire. His tone indicated that if she but wished for them to be, he would make it so.

She closed her eyes for a moment and let the wind whip through her hair. Then a smile played across her lips. "No," she finally decided, opening her eyes to gaze up at Bryce. "I think they might grow on me."

After hours of touring the grounds and witnessing much of what the palace had to offer, Talia was more in awe of her surroundings than ever before. "It's like a small city behind these gates," she said. The Comforts were restricted to their living quarters and surrounding courtyard. They weren't permitted to move about freely, more for their own protection than anything else.

"Maybe I'm just used to it. Sometimes I feel like this place is closing in on me," Bryce admitted, and the comment struck Talia as odd. "Should we get something to eat?" he asked more cheerfully, changing the subject. Talia's stomach growled in response.

He led her to one of many kitchens in the main palace. Mounds of homemade bread lined the countertops. A kettle filled with a stew-like substance coughed and bubbled on the stove. The overall aroma was marvelous.

"Hello, Frances," Bryce spoke casually to a stout, elderly lady who stood behind the counter, rolling out dough with a large rolling pin.

"Well hello, Bry…" she started, and then spotted Talia. "Hello, sir," she said more professionally.

"Relax, Frances. She's cool," he said, reviving an old phrase that hadn't been in common use for decades.

"Talia, Frances. Frances, this is my friend Talia." Talia smiled sweetly at Frances, thankful that Bryce didn't divulge the true nature of their relationship. Then again, even she wasn't certain what the true nature of her relationship with Bryce was.

"Well, aren't you a pretty little thing?" Frances said, looking Talia up and down as she spoke. Talia blushed and thanked her for the compliment.

"Frances, whip us up one of your famous dishes," Bryce commanded in playful banter before taking Talia's hand in his and leading her to a cozy dining area with a grand, stone fireplace that stretched to the ceiling.

"Is this an actual wood-burning fireplace?" she asked, excited by seeing one for the first time.

"Yes. My mother commissioned it. She oversaw every detail."

Talia ran her fingers over the rough stone. She leaned in and inhaled deeply, smiling to herself as she breathed in the aroma of smoke and charred wood. Bryce marveled at the way she took such pleasure in the everyday things that he barely took the time to notice. He took her hand in his and led her to the table. He pulled out her chair for her, then scooted it back in as she took her seat. Resisting the urge to lean in and kiss her cheek, he took a seat across from her. Talia mimicked his movements – first plucking the napkin from the plate, unfolding it, then smoothing it out over her lap.

When Frances and a second member of the kitchen staff entered with the food, Talia felt like royalty. The table was set with fine, bone china and white linens. Generous goblets of wine were poured for her and Bryce, and there were three main courses to choose from, which Frances described in detail. Talia listened with genuine interest, although she only recognized a portion of the ingredients. "I could get used to this," she said, digging in with hungry enthusiasm once the kitchen staff left the room.

"Slow down, the food's not going anywhere," Bryce teased. She smiled at him, intrigued by how comfortable he made her feel. He prompted her to try the wine, which she declined.

"I have never tried wine before. I'm not sure how much my system could handle."

Bryce appeared shocked at her admission. "Seriously?" He grew up enjoying wine at the dinner table since the age of twelve. It was custom in his land.

"Rule number 14 for a Comfort. It is unlawful to partake of anything that will alter the mind or defile the body." Talia recited the rule with flawless execution, her tone void of any emotion.

Bryce clenched his fists from beneath the table. He wondered how many rules Talia was subjected to and the thought angered him.

"Did I do something wrong?" she asked, feeling unsettled by his change of expression.

"Of course not," he said, keeping his tone light. "I was just thinking about the things that might come out of your mouth if you *did* have some wine – it seems you have a hard-enough time reining in your thoughts as it is." He shot her a wink, putting her at ease once again.

She enjoyed the meal more than she'd enjoyed anything in recent past. She focused on Bryce, her stomach fluttering with every crooked smile and her heart melting with each story he shared. Talia was amazed at the attention Bryce centered on her. His every action demonstrated a genuine interest in learning more about her. It was both unexpected and disarming.

Back at Bryce's room, Talia returned to a state of anxiousness, unsure of what was expected of her and wishing she had drank some of the wine to settle her nerves. She was, however, pleased to see a neat, folded stack of women's clothing placed on the dresser, and several gowns laid out on the bed. A row of women's shoes lined the floor below the dresser.

"Was this your doing?" she gushed, already knowing the answer. Bryce smiled, but didn't respond. Talia selected one of the nightgowns from the pile of clothing and headed towards the powder room.

Emerging several minutes later, outfitted in a new nightgown and face scrubbed clean of makeup, Talia approached the bed. Bryce was already lying down, fully dressed and stretched out on top of the covers. He was reviewing the paperwork from earlier and, to Talia's disappointment, didn't appear to notice when she entered the room.

"Is there more to that nightgown?" he asked, arching an eyebrow but still not looking up from what he was reading.

Talia smiled in smug satisfaction, realizing that he actually had noticed her come in and pleased that choosing the shortest nightgown from the pile incited a reaction. She stretched out on the bed next to him, also remaining above the covers. The night air was chilly, and she longed for the warmth of the blankets, but she was determined to seduce Bryce before he could send her back to live with the other seasoned Comforts.

"Aren't you cold?" he asked, putting down his paperwork and turning to look at her. He found it difficult to keep his eyes on her face instead of her long, slender legs.

"No," she lied while doing her best to keep her teeth from chattering. Saying nothing, Bryce sat up and grabbed a throw blanket from the foot of the bed and draped it over her. She tried to hide her disappointment as she snuggled closer to him.

"What should we do now?" she crooned.

Bryce arranged the paperwork into a neat stack and placed it on the nightstand. He gave the blanket a playful tug, inching towards Talia so that his arm was below the covers. His fingertips skimmed across her bare thigh. "What would you like to do?" he taunted.

Her heartbeat quickened, and her breathing became raspy. She reached for his hand and brought it up to her lips, kissing his fingertips. Despite her inexperience, she had been trained on how to please a man. All the Comforts had. One of the first lessons was to feign desire. It played to a nobleman's ego. Only now Talia didn't need to feign her desire. It burned inside her, scorching her very soul.

"Kiss me," she said, staring up at Bryce with her bright blue eyes. He held back. He knew what she was doing – he wasn't a fool. He couldn't blame her. After all, she was doing what she needed to survive. But he didn't want to take her that way. It felt wrong. "Please, kiss me," she said again.

This time Bryce didn't hesitate. He placed his right hand behind her slender neck and dropped his left hand to her waist as he drew her closer, leaning in to place his mouth on hers. She tasted good. God help him, he wanted her. He wrestled with his conscience as his tongue swept inside her mouth. Talia moaned softly, surprised by the rapture of the kiss and the desire it stirred within her.

Without warning, Bryce removed his hand from her waist and pulled away. Talia was breathless and confused. "What's wrong?" she asked, panting.

"Nothing," he said, rising out of bed and crossing the room to a small, wooden cabinet on the wall. He opened the cabinet door, taking out a bottle of brandy and two small glasses. He poured himself a drink and drained the glass in a single swig. He then refilled his glass, poured brandy into a second glass, and turned to face Talia – a drink in each hand.

He slowly walked back to the bed, offering Talia a glass. "I don't drink," she reminded him, but she took the glass anyways. Bryce noticed that her hands shook. He lifted his glass to hers in salute and held her gaze as he lifted his glass to his lips. She mimicked his movements, taking a small swig of the brandy and making a face. "Gross," she said. Bryce laughed.

Talia finished her glass, hoping the strange, bitter liquid would lessen the sting of his rejection. She wanted to ask what she did wrong, but her pride wouldn't let her. Bryce sat down next to her on the bed. "Do you want me to have dessert brought up for us?" he asked. Truth be told, food was the last thing on his mind.

"If you want," she shrugged. She knew her tone was as bitter as her drink, but she couldn't help it. Tears stung her eyes, and she rose from the bed. This time it was her turn to visit the liquor cabinet. She searched through its contents until she found a pretty, pink mixture. She poured a large glass and began to gulp it down – barely noticing its acrid taste.

"Easy," Bryce told her. And at once he was at her side, taking the glass from her hand. He placed it on the bar beneath the cabinet and pulled her close. "You are so beautiful."

Apparently not beautiful enough, she thought to herself. She pulled away from him but did her best to smile at his questioning look. "Dessert actually sounds good," she lied. "Something with chocolate in it, perhaps?"

He nodded and called in the order. He knew he'd done the right thing for Talia, so why did it make him feel so damn miserable?

Bryce studied Talia while she polished off her dessert. He resisted the urge to lick the chocolate from her fingertips or explore how the sugar tasted on her pouty lips. "That was to die for," she said. She was glowing with delight.

"An old family recipe," he told her.

"Seriously?"

"No, kidding. It's from the bakery just outside the palace walls."

Talia giggled. Bryce loved to watch her laugh. She seemed so care-free, so at ease. "Is that the dessert you had in mind?" he teased, and Talia flushed three shades of crimson.

CHAPTER 6

BEING AWAY FROM TALIA while he returned to his everyday business affairs was hard for Bryce. During one of his humdrum meetings, he found his thoughts wandering to her. This was not something he was accustomed to. He was known for being all-business and never felt the need to make time for a relationship. His subjects noticed the change in him and exchanged concerned looks when his back was turned.

Between meetings, Bryce scrawled a message on a small piece of paper, folded it in half, and handed it to one of his servants. "Please deliver this to my room."

Talia grew impatient waiting for Bryce to return. Although seeing him was the highlight of each day, she wasn't sure how long she would be content with waiting around in his room day after day until he had time for her. And more importantly, she wasn't sure how long Bryce would be satisfied with the arrangement. She would have to act quickly if she was going to coax him into sleeping with her. She couldn't bear the thought of losing her virginity to anyone else. She would need to seduce Bryce; she didn't have much choice. However, her many attempts had proven unsuccessful.

The knock at the door startled her, and she crept over to stare through the peephole. By the attire of her visitor, she surmised that he must be one of Bryce's servants. Tentatively, she opened the door to him. "May I help you?"

"I have a message to deliver to you," the man said. His tone reflected a combination of nervousness and confusion at Talia's presence in Bryce's bedchamber.

"Thank you," she told him, taking the folded slip of paper and closing the door. She smiled when she read the note.

Dearest Talia,

I hope you are not too bored waiting for me. I have been thinking about you all day. I've been thinking about…dessert.

Yours,

Bryce

The note was neatly printed. Its contents: maddeningly confusing. The words took Talia's breath away. "Yours," Bryce wrote. How badly she wished that were true.

When Bryce knocked on the door that evening, Talia flung it open, wrapping her arms around him before he had a chance to refuse her. Although it was only half past six, she was already in her nightgown. It was the only prodding he needed. He began to kiss her, lacing his fingers through her hair as they moved together towards the bed. He kicked the bedroom door closed – shutting them in from the rest of the world.

They fell together onto the bed, Bryce kissing Talia's neck while she moaned softly in response. He paused long enough to trace her lips with his thumb while he searched for the strength to stop himself from what he already knew he was going to do. She grabbed his right hand and skimmed her lips across his fingertips. She moved his hand down to her breasts.

He gasped, both surprised and pleased with her boldness. "Remember, we don't have to do anything you don't want to," he told her, but Talia smiled sweetly at him, prodding him to continue.

Sitting up in bed, Bryce maneuvered her onto his lap so that she was facing him. She wrapped her legs around him. He cradled her face in his hands, pulling her close to kiss her again. Heat coursed through Talia's body when she felt his tongue sweep into her mouth. He'd never kissed her like this before, and the feeling far surpassed anything she had imagined.

It was Bryce who pulled away, pushing the hair out of Talia's face so he could study her expression. "We can stop anytime you want to. Just tell me, okay?"

"I don't want you to stop," she whispered hoarsely. Her intent over the past few days was to trick him into taking her virginity, but now Talia wanted so much more – she desperately wanted Bryce to make love to her. She longed for him and hoped with everything within her that he felt the same.

Bryce wrestled with his conscience. He knew Talia had been trying to seduce him ever since she realized the next nobleman might not be as gentle with her as he would be. She was far too innocent and honest to hide her intentions – they were written all over her face. But now, her desire seemed genuine and she had matched his kisses with equal fervor. He questioned whether the passions he felt radiating from her were nothing more than wishful thinking manifested by his own longing, but his need for her consumed him and despite his principles, he succumbed to his desires.

This time when Bryce kissed her, he held nothing back. The taste of her was intoxicating. Although she wasn't the first virgin he had been with, she somehow seemed sweeter – more innocent. He slipped the nightgown over her head and discarded it on the floor. Talia's nipples hardened in response to the cold, and he leaned in to kiss each one; his tongue tormenting, teasing.

Talia responded with a deep sigh. Her fingers drifted to Bryce's shirt, loosening each button before moving on to his belt buckle. "I can do it faster, if you'll allow me," he whispered in her ear, nibbling on her earlobe.

Nodding in agreement, Talia let go of his belt, but not before she stroked his inner thigh. Growling with desire, he rose from the bed, stripping off his garments one by one until he stood before Talia unclothed. This time she did not divert her eyes. She stared at Bryce in all his glory.

"Last chance to turn back," he said, but he hoped with everything within him that she wouldn't change her mind.

In response, Talia motioned him towards her with her index finger. Her body was trembling. Not with fear, although she was a little scared of what was to come, but with deep desire. Bryce climbed into bed, stretching his body over hers.

"I need you," Bryce whispered in Talia's ear. Something about her made him feel vulnerable – a sensation that he wasn't used to, and he wasn't all too sure how he felt about it.

Talia placed her hands on his bare chest, gliding her fingers down his torso and letting them rest below his navel before mustering the courage to explore further. She wasn't sure what she was doing, but her curious hands drifted below his waist. Bryce sucked in his breath as she grasped his swollen manhood with her inquisitive hands.

"You keep this up *ameerah*, and it's going to be an early night," he teased, pulling her right hand to his lips. "How about if you let me pleasure you for a while?"

Squirming with anticipation, Talia ran her fingers through Bryce's hair as he caressed her inner thigh. His hands trailed up her thigh until his fingertips grazed the hair protecting her womanhood. He stroked her femininity with his thumb. She felt herself grow hot and moist. An unfamiliar ache stirred in the area Bryce was touching.

Without warning, he dipped one finger inside her, then withdrew it slowly. He repeated the movement, studying Talia's reaction to be sure he wasn't hurting her. She sighed and instinctively lifted her hips towards him, as if begging for more. This time Bryce used two fingers, moving in and out while Talia urged him to continue.

"Are you ready?" he asked. Talia nodded – her eyes wide and innocent. "I'll try my best, but this is going to hurt a little. The pain won't last long though, okay?"

"I want you so bad," she whispered in response.

With great patience and restraint, Bryce eased inside her. Talia winced and closed her eyes. Bryce froze, giving her a chance to recover. "Open your eyes, Talia," he ordered.

She opened her eyes and stared at him. She was so innocently beautiful. He could hardly wait to push himself inside her, but he knew he needed to be patient. He placed his hand on her soft cheek, tracing her lips and stroking her jawline with his thumb. "Just look at me, okay. It'll be okay." Talia nodded again, and Bryce could tell she trusted him. He eased in further, pressing his lips to her ear and reassuring her that the pain would pass. Once he was inside, his movements were slow, gentle.

At first Talia did not move. She didn't close her eyes, but Bryce could tell it was uncomfortable for her. Tortured at the thought of hurting her, he wondered if he should stop, but it was Talia who urged him to keep going. As he continued to move within her, her body started to respond. She lifted her hips toward him, taking him in further and moaning with desire rather than pain.

"You're lovely," he told her, delighted that she was starting to feel pleasure from his deep thrusts.

Talia smiled and allowed herself to give in completely to him. She wrapped her legs around him and began to match his maddening rhythm. A deep, urgent need was building inside her that she didn't quite understand. It was as if she was striving for something just out of reach.

She dug her nails into his back, begging him to release her; from what, she wasn't sure.

Bryce fought the urge to drive harder, faster – but he wanted Talia to orgasm first. He wanted to be hard inside her as she climaxed. Her breathing accelerated, and he could tell she was getting close.

Loving how he felt inside her, Talia sighed and pleaded for more. Bryce's pace quickened with each thrust. His mouth closed over hers, muffling her passionate cries as she climaxed. He felt the pulsing from deep within when she reached her peak. Her pleasure was his undoing and he found his own release.

Easing his way out of her, Bryce collapsed next to Talia. He cradled her in his arms and kissed her shoulder. She didn't move, and he felt the guilt wash over him. Had it been wrong to make love to her? Perhaps he'd misread her desire.

He sat up in bed to get a better look at her. He expected to see tears, but instead he found her smiling. Her hair was disheveled, and beads of perspiration lined her forehead, but she looked serene. "That was... that was..." She flushed, lost for words.

"Are you alright?" he asked, prepared to hate himself if he'd hurt her.

"Yes. More than alright. I just never thought it would be like that." She sighed in contentment and cuddled up to him. "Was it... okay for you?" she asked, self-conscious of her inexperience.

"You were amazing," he told her, kissing the top of her head and exulting in her scent. He meant it. She had more passion and fire than any woman he'd ever been with.

Talia smiled shyly, pleased with the compliment. She snuggled closer to him, forgetting the wall of pillows that had formed a barrier between them just days before. For the moment, she felt at ease.

Bryce watched her fall asleep, marveling at how peaceful she looked curled up beside him, her plump lips parted slightly, and her dark ringlets splayed across the pillow. He reached over to sweep the hair from her forehead but stopped himself. He could feel himself starting to care for her and knew he couldn't allow it. He refused to be weak like his father, relying on Comforts to keep the loneliness at bay.

The prince still recalled bits and pieces from his early childhood. The memories were hazy, but he remembered his mother begging for his father to stay home instead of seeking pleasure with other women. Bryce could still hear his mother's soft cries from behind her bedroom door. He could still recall sneaking out of his room to witness his father staggering in late, drunk, and smelling like booze and perfume. It was during one of those late nights that Bryce swore he would never be like the man he saw stumbling home and causing his loved ones such undeserved pain.

The prince considered all these things while he contemplated his next move. His heart ached in his chest as he draped an arm around Talia's sleeping form. He pulled her close and buried his face in her hair. He told himself that he had to send her back, convincing himself that it was the right thing to do – for both of them.

CHAPTER 7

WHEN MORNING CAME, Talia awoke to find she was alone. The room was tidy, except for the bed she slept in and an absurdly large suitcase by the bedroom door. The clothes Bryce ordered brought up for her no longer lined the dresser and, with a sinking heart, she realized what was happening. Bryce was done with her, and she was being sent back.

A young handmaid knocked softly on the door and entered without waiting for a response. She handed Talia a luxurious, terrycloth robe and told her that a guard would be arriving in precisely thirty minutes to escort her back to her quarters. Refusing to cry, Talia lifted her chin and climbed out of bed with all the dignity she could muster. She slipped into the soft robe and headed to the bathroom to grab a quick shower.

Once inside the shower, she let herself shed a few tears, hoping the water from the showerheads would mask her cries. When the soapy water ran down her body and hit between her thighs, she cringed. The sting of the soap was a brutal reminder of the night prior and how, like a fool, she had let herself believe that it was anything more to the prince than just another casual tryst.

Talia knew she shouldn't be bitter. Bryce had been so kind to her during their brief time together. She had no right to assume he would keep her around any longer, not when he could have any woman he desired. She wanted to be grateful for the way he had so gently guided her to womanhood, but all she felt was deep sorrow and a puzzling feeling of rejection.

No longer wanting to wallow in self-pity, Talia manually shut off the faucets and stepped out of the shower. She grabbed a towel from the hook and wrapped herself in it, taking small comfort in how the cloth felt against her damp skin. On the bathroom counter was a floor-length, honey-colored dress and a new pair of panties and she realized the handmaid must have laid them out. She dressed quickly, wanting to leave Bryce's living quarters before he came back. She wanted her last physical moments with him to be a happy memory.

When she returned to the bedroom, a guard was standing by the door, the large suitcase in his hand. She suspected the suitcase held all the dresses and elegant nightgowns Bryce had given her and she was grateful she would at least have something to remember him by. She was also grateful that it wasn't the same guard who had brought her to Bryce's room on the night of the Harvest Ball. That one had been surly and pompous. This one seemed pleasant and humble. She smiled at him, as if this was another ordinary day, and allowed him to escort her to the new place she would now call home.

The guard, who introduced himself as Chadwick, brought Talia to a row of three large, multi-storied dwellings outside the main palace. The dwellings shared a cobblestone courtyard, with tulip-lined flagstone pathways leading to each structure. The buildings reminded Talia of the fraternity houses she had read about in the Grand Americas. Each was painted a distinct color, trimmed in a brilliant white, and boasted a modest-sized, white painted deck and a faux wooden door. A small, wooden sign etched with a combination of numbers and letters was mounted on each building. On the first building, which was painted in brick red, the sign read "A: 18 – 21." "B: 22 – 25" was displayed on the cream-colored building, and "C: 26 – 29" was displayed on the pale-yellow building next to it.

Talia learned that Building A would be her new home and things began to make sense. The numbers indicated the age of the Comforts living within. If she did the math correctly, at fifteen Comforts turned out per year, each building would house approximately sixty women. Chadwick knocked twice, then opened the door to Building A. A rather rotund but handsome woman met them at the entryway and grabbed the enormous suitcase from Chadwick before dismissing him with a grunt. The guard offered Talia a nod before walking away, closing the door behind him.

"I'm Sasha, the house matron," the woman said, turning to Talia. "Come with me and I'll show you to your room." Talia followed obediently. The inside of Building A resembled a hotel with its massive lobby, elongated hallways, and numbered doors leading to identically-sized rooms. She passed a few ladies in the first hallway, but nobody she recognized. She followed Sasha up a narrow flight of stairs to the second floor. They took a right down one more corridor, before coming to a stop.

"Here it is," Sasha announced, using a keycard to open a door marked A22.

The furnishings in Talia's newly assigned room were sparse and included a twin-sized bed, a modest nightstand, a folding chair, a faux-wooden dresser, and not much else. A tattered curtain cloaked the small window. Sasha set down the heavy suitcase with a grunt, handed Talia the keycard, and excused herself from the room. It was not until Talia was convinced she was alone that she finally broke down. She had felt so certain she could trust Bryce. Now she felt betrayed.

She allowed herself to cry for precisely thirty minutes. Then, like a switch, she turned it off. She rose from the bed, wiped away her tears, and examined her reflection in the mirror above the dresser. Once she was confident her eyes no longer looked red and puffy, she plastered a smile on her face and began to move about her room. Her surroundings were vastly different from the room she'd shared with Bryce. The walls were void of tapestries. The floor was made of ceramic tile rather than fine marble. She put away her meager belongings, making the space her own.

She couldn't bring herself to join the other Comforts, not yet. At lunchtime, there was a brisk knock at her door, and someone left a tray of food for her in the hallway – a ham sandwich with potato chips and a glass of cold milk. Talia nibbled at the sandwich, washed it down with the milk, then returned the tray to the hallway with the half-eaten sandwich hidden beneath a crumpled napkin. She wasn't so lucky at dinner time, but she didn't have much of an appetite anyway. She went to bed early; alone and confused.

CHAPTER 8

AS MUCH AS BRYCE tried, he couldn't concentrate on anything that day. He was also snappy with anyone he encountered. Puzzled by his less-than-pleasant mood, his constituents gave him a wide berth. Something was gnawing at him, and the more he tried to convince himself that it wasn't about Talia, the more remorseful he felt for sending her away – and the more he longed for her.

She had submitted herself so freely to him. She had trusted him with her innocence, and he shattered that trust by abandoning her the next morning. He felt as if he'd offered her up like a sacrificial lamb and it twisted his stomach into knots.

After a long day, he went back to his bedchamber alone. When he opened his bedroom door he half expected to see Talia waiting for him, hands on her hips and ready to scold him for having dismissed her so rudely. Instead the room was empty, which coincidentally was how he felt. Empty.

Talia didn't sleep well. Her attempts to push Bryce out of her mind were a failure. He consumed her every thought. The fire in his eyes; the reverence of his touch. She remembered all too well how it felt to have his strong hands on her body – holding her, caressing her. She could still feel his lips on hers, hear the sweet things he'd whispered when they'd made love. When she did sleep, she dreamed of him, reliving every tender moment they spent together. It was maddening.

By the next morning, the pit in her stomach had grown but she did her best to put on a brave face. She joined the other Comforts for breakfast in the large dining room, careful to seat herself between two ladies she didn't know. Her disheveled appearance and solemn disposition were enough to keep most questions at bay, but not the inquisitive and sympathetic glances. She ate in silence and pretended not to notice the gazes from the other Comforts.

After breakfast she cleared her plate, disposing of the scarcely touched food, and slipped away to the drawing room. She knew she should reconnect with some of the girls she had grown close to over the past two years. The unselfish thing would be to at least confirm everyone was alright. But Talia wasn't up for being selfless. Not today.

At first blush, the drawing room appeared empty and Talia headed for the leather sofa to settle in with a book. She was in the center of the room before she noticed a Comfort she recognized as Rachel sitting alone in the far corner. Rachel had always been quiet, but sweet. When Talia approached her, she noticed Rachel's blackened eye and cut lip. Her jaw tightened in anger as she rushed to sit next to her.

"Are you okay?" she asked. Rachel remained silent, but her lip trembled.

"Kaden bid on me, right after that prince asked for you," she finally said. Her tone was bitter, and Talia sensed that Rachel blamed her somehow.

"I'm so sorry," Talia told her. She felt angry and guilty, and selfishly, a little relieved.

Rachel began to cry. "We all thought that it would be *you* Kaden would bid on," she wailed, burying her head in her hands.

Talia wrapped a protective arm around her shoulders. Her thoughts drifted to Bryce and her bitterness was temporarily replaced with gratitude. He had saved her that day, even if her heart and pride were paying a high price for it now. "I'm going to try and fix this," she told her, although she wasn't sure how.

Rachel sprang from her chair. "Nobody can fix this," she hissed, fighting back more tears as she fled from the room.

Talia sank onto the couch. She hugged her knees to her chest as she tried to process what she was feeling.

Seven o'clock in the evening was selection time for the occupants of all three houses. Talia learned this on the first night but had been spared from having to join the others. Sasha, the house matron, must have decided she was too much of an emotional wreck to be a good companion to anyone. Today she would not be as lucky. The Comforts were given an hour to look presentable, then they all formed a line in the outer courtyard. The noblemen rarely came themselves to make their selection, especially since most of them were married. Instead, they sent a trusted servant, who often came armed with a list of specifications. Some servants were familiar with their master's preferences and no list was required.

Talia inserted herself in line amongst a couple of ladies she didn't know. Her heart hammered in her chest and her throat felt dry. She did notice that Rachel wasn't amongst the Comforts and it gave her some relief that the house matron was giving the poor girl time to recover. Then again, Sasha probably realized the noblemen wouldn't want anyone with a bruised face.

One by one the Comforts were scrutinized and, if they met the list of criteria, were chosen. Tall, blue eyes, long hair, curly hair, medium build… check, check. Talia felt like she was being selected from a tray of desserts and her fists balled in anger at her sides.

One servant was eyeing her too long. Her stomach flip-flopped, fearing she knew what that meant. Fear crept up her spine as she wondered what features she possessed that would be her curse. She lowered her eyes and concentrated on looking dull. "This one," the servant called out, pointing at Talia. She imagined it was a rare moment of power the man was feeling, summoning her in such a way, and she glared in his direction while she did her best to swallow the lump forming in her throat.

Sasha motioned the servant over to where she sat perched in the far corner of the courtyard. The pair appeared to have a heated exchange, which ended with the servant walking back to the line and selecting one of the ladies further down from where Talia stood. The woman resembled Talia but appeared to be a few years older.

Talia was relieved, and to her surprise and some resolution of her guilt, the woman selected appeared relieved as well. Maybe it was a matter of pride for the woman, reassurance she was still pretty enough to be chosen despite the newer crop. Talia was confused by the exchange. She wondered what Sasha had said that had changed the servant's mind. Whatever it was, she was grateful. Although she knew it was inevitable, she couldn't imagine what it would be like to have another man put his hands on her and was thankful that, at least for tonight, she wouldn't have to find out.

At seven-thirty, the nightly selection process came to a close and the remaining Comforts filed back inside their assigned houses. Talia felt like she dodged a bullet, but most of the women appeared at ease, as if it didn't matter one way or another to them if they were chosen. Veronica, one of the Comforts Talia had befriended through the years, tried to make eye contact with her, but Talia ignored her and headed straight for Sasha, who was making her way to the kitchen.

"Sasha, can I speak with you for a moment?"

Sasha grabbed Talia's arm and pulled her aside so they were tucked away in the corner of the room. She glanced around, then spoke, keeping her voice low. "Don't ask. Just be happy with the outcome, and don't ask." Then she released Talia's arm and walked away.

Talia stood alone, bewildered. Perhaps Bryce had interfered. Or perhaps Kaden was saving her for himself. She shuddered at that last thought. Drained by the encounter, and emotions running high, she wandered upstairs to get ready for bed.

Once she returned to her room, she slipped out of her dress and into one of the pretty nightgowns Bryce had given her. She missed him.

Part of her hated him, but mostly she just missed him. Grabbing her hair brush, she sat on the edge of the bed and began to brush out her hair. And with every stroke of the brush, another tear of bitterness fell from her face.

CHAPTER 9

BRYCE TOSSED AND TURNED for yet another night, but sleep continued to elude him. He pictured Talia with another man and the thought sickened him. Sure, he had kept the other noblemen away for now – ordering the house matron to turn away any would-be suitors. But that would only work for so long. He couldn't get over the guilt of abandoning her and no longer trusted his decision to send her away.

At three in the morning he could stand it no longer. He summoned a servant to his room. He barked out his orders, demanding that the man carry them out at once. He was certain the servant took him for a crazy person or a sex addict – perhaps both.

Talia was dreaming about Bryce when she was shaken awake by a reed-thin, older man she'd never seen before. Her first instinct was to scream, but the man gently covered her mouth with his hand and whispered that he was there on official business for the prince, who had demanded Talia's immediate company.

She was furious. How dare the prince insult her by demanding sex with her after he so carelessly tossed her aside just days before. "And if I refuse to go?" she asked.

"Oh, Miss, no one refuses such a thing," the man warned her.

Certain he was right, Talia knew she should follow orders, but she was still smarting from the pain of Bryce's dismissal. She scrambled out of bed in anger, not bothering to cover up with a robe. She saw the shocked stare from the servant at the sight of her short nightgown.

"Listen here," she told the man, pretending not to notice his stunned expression. "All that the prince wants is a little late-night tryst. Although he seems to have given you my name, I am quite certain it's because my name is the only one he knows amongst the Comforts and the specifics of his request were merely out of convenience as opposed to any real desire for me personally. I am sure there are plenty of girls who would be more than willing to take my place. I suggest you go find one of them." And with that, she ushered the dazed man towards the door, closing it in his face.

Talia tried to fall back to sleep, but realizing what a mistake she just made, she felt a sinking in her gut. She was angry with Bryce, but she didn't want him to replace her with someone else. She thought of him taking another Comfort to his bed and it made her nauseous. The next girl would probably be more willing, perhaps better at lovemaking than she had been, and Bryce might keep her around. As the thoughts bounced around in her head, the hot tears streamed down her face and fell on her pillow.

While she laid in bed feeling sorry for herself, her somber thoughts were interrupted by a knock on the door. She flew to the door, prepared to give the servant a thorough tongue-lashing, although she was relieved at the prospect of another chance. She threw open the door, still not bothering to put on a robe.

"Hello, Talia," Bryce said, trying to be pleasant. She blinked twice to be sure she wasn't dreaming, and the guard at Bryce's side slinked away, leaving Talia to fend for herself.

"So, what, you couldn't sleep and just needed another roll in the sheets?" she hissed. She could feel her bottom lip tremble, so she sucked it in before Bryce could notice. She didn't want to give him the satisfaction.

"It's not like that," he said, keeping his tone even.

"Oh, really? Then tell me what it's like." She knew she was flirting with danger by being so insubordinate, but she was far too angry and wounded to care.

Bryce ignored her and stepped into the room. He pushed past her, making his way to her small closet and producing a robe from where she had discarded it on the floor. "Put this on," he ordered, and this time Talia thought it wise to obey.

Taking her by the arm, Bryce escorted her through the streets, to the palace, and back to his room. Talia was too confused and nervous to do anything but be led along in silence. Chadwick, the guard, remained a respectful distance behind them.

Once behind the closed doors of his living quarters, Bryce pulled Talia into his arms and kissed her, hard. At first, she fought to resist him, but soon realized her efforts were pointless and a matter of pride. She desired him, and despite her tormented thoughts, she found herself kissing him back.

"Oh, my beautiful Talia, I should never have sent you away."

"Why did you?" she asked, pulling back from him, but softening her voice. "What did I do?" Her throat felt tight and her words sounded strangled.

"Nothing. You were perfect. I just… I shouldn't get involved with you. I thought it best to walk away before things got too complicated between us."

"Things don't have to get complicated," Talia said, her voice barely above a whisper.

"Oh, Talia, they already are." And although he knew that he shouldn't, he gathered her up in his arms and brought her over to his bed. He set her down and gazed into her bright blue eyes. "Did you feel okay the next morning?" he asked, wondering if she had any adverse effects from their love-making.

"I was a tiny bit sore, so the shower hurt a little," she admitted, lowering her eyes as the heat crept up her neck.

Bryce felt a new level of self-loathing. Not only had he hurt her physically, he hadn't even bothered to stick around the next morning to find out how she was. He thought his presence would be too painful – for her, for him – but now he realized she must have thought him a coward.

"I'm so sorry, *ameerah*," he told her, pushing back her robe and skimming his fingers over her bare shoulder. Talia loved it when he called her that. Her anger partially subsiding, she reassured him that she felt fine.

"We don't have to do anything," he continued. "Just as long as you stay here with me, it will be enough."

"But, I want you to make love to me," Talia confessed. "Please, Bryce, just one more time before you send me away again." Her eyes were wide, innocent and her throat constricted with the fear of rejection.

Bryce planted a tender kiss above her collar line. "I have no intentions of sending you away again," he murmured as his lips brushed against her skin.

Her heartbeat quickened. "So, you... you want me to stay?"

"I *need* you to stay," he corrected her. He touched her face and was surprised by the moisture on her cheek. He wiped her tears away with this thumb as his mouth claimed hers.

Feverish hands fumbled to remove clothing and the pair fell into bed, entangled in each other. This time when Bryce entered her, Talia didn't feel any pain, only warmth and desire. He was patient, compassionate, and generous – and with every tender kiss, her feelings for him deepened. She was falling in love with him, this much she knew, but as much as she wanted to tell him, she had promised that things didn't have to be complicated. She knew confessing she loved him would muddle things for him, so she kept the sentiment to herself.

"I missed you," she told him instead.

"I missed you too," he admitted, and Talia told herself that, for now, it would have to be enough.

CHAPTER 10

EARLY THE NEXT MORNING Talia woke with a start. Filled with dread, she rolled over, fearing she would once again find Bryce's side of the bed empty. Instead, he lay sleeping beside her. Relieved, she closed her eyes and sank her head back on the pillow. She resisted the urge to grasp his hand in hers to ensure he couldn't leave. Bryce reached out in his sleep and draped an arm across her body. Content, Talia drifted back to sleep.

When she awoke once more, the sunlight was peeking through the partially open curtains and Bryce was already awake and showered. He nudged her awake, placing a tray of food in front of her. "Breakfast?"

"Why are you spoiling me today?" she asked, sitting up in bed and breathing in the delicious smell of waffles with homemade whipped cream and huckleberry compote.

"I should have done this a few days ago," he said. "I'm so sorry, Talia."

"Stop, you have done so much for me already. Really – more than you know." She chose not to mention Rachel's ordeal with Kaden. It made her feel too guilty. She remembered the final months leading up to the Harvest Ball. Kaden had become more forceful, hanging out more than usual, and leaning in too close to be interpreted as anything other than sinister. Looking back, she realized he may have planned to take her before the ball. He may have figured he could outbid the others later and no one would be the wiser. Her stomach lurched at the thought. She had been right to lock her door each evening. On some occasions, she had propped her chair under the door handle or slid her dresser in front of the door.

"Honestly Bryce, you have nothing to be sorry for," she repeated.

He didn't agree. In his mind, he had a long way to go before he rectified how he'd treated her, but he kept the thought to himself. "What would you like to do today?" he asked, changing the subject and taking a seat at the foot of the bed.

"What would you like to do?"

"Well, I already promised a friend of mine that I would go quail hunting with him, so whatever you want to do, you're free to do."

She tried to hide her disappointment. It was unrealistic to assume Bryce could hang out with her every day. "I might just go back to my place."

"Your place is here," he said, cutting her off. His tone held a warning.

She wanted to argue, but she held her tongue. She didn't want to spoil what little time she and Bryce had together. "Well, I just meant I could go visit some of my friends. You forget that I spent every day for the past two years with some of these ladies. I wouldn't mind hanging out with them while you're busy. I didn't have much time to reconnect with any of them during my brief stay." She looked wounded. The painful memories of the past two days were still fresh.

A knock on the door interrupted their conversation. Talia pulled the covers up to her chin, then nodded at Bryce that she was ready, assuming it was one of the servants coming back to haul away the empty trays of food. Her stomach lurched when Kaden Huff entered the room. He strode in with casual indifference, casting a glance in Talia's direction. Her body broke out in a cold sweat.

Was Bryce about to commit the ultimate betrayal and hand her over to Kaden? It was obvious they were friends – perhaps Kaden had made the request. She felt ill, but she squared her shoulders and snuck a pleading glance at Bryce, who was preoccupied with finding his boots.

"You ready to go?" Kaden asked, directing his question to Bryce.

Talia let out a slow, raspy sigh of relief. Kaden was the hunting buddy. She might have guessed that.

"Yep, I just have to grab the rest of my hunting gear from the closet." Bryce disappeared around the corner, oblivious to Talia's growing discomfort.

"So, my little flower snagged herself a prince," Kaden chided once he was certain the prince was out of earshot. Talia balled up her fists from beneath the covers. She looked straight ahead, doing her best to ignore him as she concentrated on returning her breathing pattern to normal.

"You know, I had every intention of bidding on you. I guess I'll just have to settle for seconds."

She was about to debate Kaden's disgusting words when Bryce walked back into the room. "You ready?" Bryce asked. He walked to his dresser and retrieved a large, fixed-blade hunting knife from his sock drawer.

"Let's do it," Kaden responded, his demeanor returning to all smiles and charm.

Talia felt the bile rise in her throat at observing the close friendship the two men shared. "You going to be okay here without me?" Bryce asked her, fastening the knife to the belt around his waist. With all the grace she could muster, Talia smiled and told both men to have a good time. Her smile was forced, and her skin felt tight against the unnatural expression.

Bryce sat on the edge of the bed and stared longingly at her. Sensing that he was a third wheel, Kaden excused himself from the room. Bryce nuzzled Talia's neck, then pressed his lips to hers. Her hands were still shaking from her encounter with Kaden, so she kept them tucked under the covers. "That's your friend?" she asked, unable to stop herself.

"We've been friends for years, pretty much since we were in diapers. Why?"

"No reason." She did her best to sound nonchalant, but her words were high-pitched and forced. "Good luck on your hunt." Bryce could tell there was something she wasn't saying, but not wanting to leave his friend waiting in the hall any longer, he kissed her one last time and headed out.

Alone with her thoughts, Talia pushed Kaden out of her mind and set out to get ready for her day. Now that she was certain Kaden wouldn't be around, she was even more excited about seeing her friends. She selected the least flashy outfit she could find from those Bryce had given her – a teal silk blouse, a gray, flowy skirt, and black flats.

When she stepped out of the prince's bedchamber and into the hallway, she was startled by a man's voice. "Where would you like to go, Miss?" She glanced to her left and noticed a guard stationed on a chair outside the door. Talia recognized him as the same guard who accompanied Bryce the previous evening when he'd come to retrieve her. He was handsome, she realized for the first time – in a boyish sort of way. Blonde, clean-cut, medium build; he looked like a Boy Scout (or what she imagined a Boy Scout might look like).

"Chadwick, right?"

"Yes, Miss," he said, standing to his feet.

"Talia," she corrected. "I'm okay, I'm just going back to my quarters."

"I'll walk you there." He offered Talia his arm.

"No, I'll be fine. I know the way."

"I'm sorry, Miss," Chadwick said, ignoring her request for him to call her by name. "I've been given strict orders to escort you anywhere you would like to go."

Talia felt annoyed, but she took his arm and allowed herself to be escorted to her destination. When they reached Building A, she knocked on the door, even though she knew she was well within her rights to be there. This was her home too. A girl she recognized as Sephora answered the door. Talia was relieved to see that Sephora looked well. Her exotic beauty and gentle nature were unspoiled.

Sephora offered Talia a warm embrace, then slung an arm around her shoulder and led her to the main living room. Chadwick followed close behind. Most of the Comforts were awake, mingling between the living room and the kitchen. Everyone was friendly and seemed in good spirits, something that gave Talia a sense of relief, and although she knew it was temporary, her guilt absconded. She wasn't certain how the rest of the women her age had fared in the days since the Harvest Ball and she had been in no condition during her previous stay to find out.

"By the way, the girls and I wanted to thank you for getting us the pool table and for the new sofa in the sitting room," Sephora told her as they took their seats in the living room.

"Pardon?" Talia was taken back.

"Oh, don't be modest, we know you arranged it. They arrived just after you left."

Talia smiled to herself, realizing it must have been Bryce's doing. The man was thoughtful without taking credit. She glanced over at Chadwick, who confirmed her suspicions with a wink and a nod. "It was nothing," she finally said.

Talia's visit was pleasant. None of the other girls had suffered the same plight poor Rachel had. They seemed to be settling into their new lives and accepting their fate. The new crop of Comforts huddled in the living room where they inundated Talia with questions about where she had been and why she had shown up again, only to be gone two days later. Talia kept her answers brief, knowing she had been luckier than most. Rachel eventually joined the group, although she didn't contribute to the conversation.

"Thank you for coming with me," she told Chadwick as they made their way back to the main palace.

"The pleasure was all mine," he said, and Talia could tell his response was genuine.

Back at Bryce's chambers, Talia showered, changed into a pale-yellow gown, and got ready to see him. She wanted to look beautiful for him, renewed in her appreciation for all he had done for her – and what he had unknowingly saved her from. When the bedroom door opened, she rushed over to it, expecting to see Bryce. Her heart leapt into her throat when she found herself standing toe-to-toe with Kaden.

"Where's Bryce?" she asked warily, taking an involuntary step backwards.

Kaden pushed his way into the bedroom. "Oh, he'll be up later. He got tied up with some business downstairs. I think he's going to be a while." As he approached her, she took another step back.

"The guards are just outside," she warned. Her eyes darted towards the open doorway.

"Actually, it seems they are with Bryce. Important business." Kaden moved in slowly, taunting her.

"You shouldn't be here," she said, but her heart was pounding hard in her chest. She'd seen Rachel's cut lip and understood how dangerous Kaden could be.

"But, yet, I *am* here. I've been waiting a long time to have you alone and to have the rights to you."

"You have no rights to me. Bryce wouldn't allow it."

"Oh, come on Talia. Don't think for a moment that he cares for you. I've seen the way he's used women in the past. Besides, I'm his oldest friend. I'm quite certain he would offer you to me if I just asked."

Kaden's words stung, and Talia sucked in her breath to recover. Before she could stop him, his large hand closed around her neck and he shoved her up against the wall. Talia's head bounced off the smooth plaster and her vision blurred. Her survival instincts kicked in and she kneed him as hard as she could. Her knee connected with his groin and he howled in pain.

Attempting to get away, she bolted for the door, but Kaden caught her by the hair, throwing her onto the bed. He tore at her clothes as he straddled her. When she screamed, his lips clamped down on hers. Talia bit him hard, tasting blood. He jerked her up by the bodice of her gown, then slapped her across the face, grazing her right eye with his open palm.

Reeling from the blow and about to lose hope that she would be able to protect herself from him, Talia heard an angry shout and felt Kaden being lifted off of her. She opened her eyes and saw Bryce tossing Kaden into the corner as if he weighed no more than a sack of potatoes. Kaden bolted from the room, and after casting a quick, angry glance in her direction, Bryce followed after him.

Alone and terrified, Talia began to shake. She realized this was only a glimpse of what Rachel had endured, and she ran to the bathroom to throw up. Leaning over the sink and splashing water in her face, she looked at her reflection in the mirror. Her dress was torn, and her hair looked wild and unkempt. A faint bruise was forming under her right eye and trailed down her cheekbone.

She thought back to the look Bryce had given her. He looked so angry. Perhaps he believed she had wanted Kaden. Or perhaps he was angry that another man had touched her, had placed his lips on hers, and he would no longer find her desirable.

"You okay?" Bryce spoke up from the doorway. Talia jumped. She had been so wrapped up in her thoughts she hadn't heard him come back in.

She rushed to his side. "I'm so sorry Bryce. I tried to stop him from kissing me. Please don't be mad." Her eyes stung with tears as the fear welled up inside her.

Bryce placed an index finger on her lips, silencing her. "Sweetie, I'm not mad at you. I am angry with myself for not seeing this coming. I knew Kaden could be somewhat of a jerk, but I never would have thought… God, I am so sorry."

He examined her torn dress, then pressed his lips to her swollen cheek. "I thought I was keeping you safe. Apparently, I can't even protect you in my own room." He pounded his fist into the wall, startling Talia, something he regretted the moment it happened.

"What did you do to Kaden?" she asked, witnessing his obvious rage.

"I couldn't find him. The little worm is hiding somewhere, but I've got people on it. They'll find him."

"I went to go see the other Comforts today," she whispered.

"I know. Chadwick told me." His tone hinted at his disapproval.

"Kaden did far worse to one of the other girls. Her name is Rachel. He bid on her that day," Talia's voice trailed off and her voice broke. "I just feel so guilty. She told me everyone expected him to bid on me." The words were painful to say aloud – fueling her guilt.

"Stop," Bryce said, sickened at the thought of Kaden having Talia instead. "Don't feel guilty," he said more softly. "I don't want you to feel anything but safe and happy."

"*You* make me feel safe and happy," she assured him, gazing up at him.

Bryce kissed her, wishing with everything within him that he deserved her kind words. But he had a dark secret, a secret about Kaden. A secret he was certain Talia would hate him for if she knew the truth.

"Want to take a shower with me?" he asked, changing the subject. "I've spent the day out in the brush, and you probably want to get cleaned up."

Talia smiled, which sent a throbbing pain across her cheek, but she did her best not to react. "I'd love to get naked with you if that's what you're asking." She flushed with shyness and excitement.

Bryce lifted her now ruined dress above her head and leaned in close to her ear. "So, what did you do when you visited your friends? Were there pillow fights?" he teased.

"No," she laughed. She removed her underneath clothes and tossed them in the corner.

The prince raised an eyebrow and wriggled out of his boots and pants. "Spin the bottle? A friendly game of Twister?" He slipped off his shirt and underwear and stood before her naked and unashamed.

Gawking at his chiseled form, Talia asked, "Do they even sell that game anymore?"

"Why?" Bryce said, pressing his body against hers. "You interested in playing? I can find out if they have any at the antique store." With one hand he swept a tendril of hair behind her ear, and with the other he squeezed her bare buttocks.

"You're such a male," she teased, grabbing his hand and coaxing him into the shower. She hadn't lied. Bryce did make her feel safe – and happy – and when his lips clamped down on hers, her recent encounter with Kaden was almost forgotten. Almost.

CHAPTER 11

"I HAVE TO GO away on business for a few days," Bryce told Talia one morning as they lounged in bed, spent from their lovemaking. Talia did her best to hide her emotions, but she felt her hands tremble and her heart flutter. This meant she would have to go back to living with the other Comforts, and although Kaden was no longer a threat, any other nobleman was.

"When will you be back?" she asked, trying to sound casual.

"Oh, probably on Wednesday."

"Well, it's about time that I went back to my living quarters anyway. I probably won't even remember which room mine is."

Bryce looked confused. "No, Talia, you will stay here. My guards can better protect you. At least one guard will be assigned to you at all times, and they know not to let anyone in here unless I specifically authorized it." He planted a kiss on her still partially swollen cheek.

"Bryce, I can't just…"

"Talia, I want you to stay with me. I told you before that I have no intention of sending you back."

She contemplated his words in silence, and the mixed emotions they stirred within her. He was giving her the rare opportunity to be his personal Comfort, meaning no other man could touch her. But now she loved him, and the thought of standing by while he eventually married and started a family with someone else sickened her. She didn't think it was something she could bear.

"That is, unless you don't want to stay with me," Bryce said, interrupting her thoughts. He sounded nervous, as if he expected her to refuse him.

"Yes, yes, I will stay," Talia said. She would do it because it made him happy, and she would work out the matters of her heart on another day.

"Good," he said, smiling. "It's settled then."

After breakfast in bed and a long, hot shower together, Bryce left Talia standing alone and naked in the bathroom, wrapped in a towel, while he stepped out of the room to finalize the security detail for his trip, and more importantly, for Talia.

She leaned in to un-fog the bathroom mirror with her hand and the mirror lit up. She was both startled and amused to discover that it was a touch screen. Several icons appeared in the corner of the screen, and a voice prompted her to choose her filter. She leaned in closer to view her options and touched the icon that looked like a feather. Her reflection in the mirror softened. Her creamy complexion looked even silkier. *Soft lens on*, the voice sounded. She smiled to herself and chose the lipstick icon instead. The reflection staring back at her was hers, but not quite. The woman in the mirror had thicker lashes, rosier cheeks, and her lips were painted red. *Glamour lens on*, the voice sounded again.

Talia was hit with a fit of the giggles as she went through each filter option. There was one that made her look leaner, while another made her look taller and more muscular.

"What is so funny?" she heard Bryce ask from the doorway. She jumped at the sound of his voice, but then turned to face him, grinning widely.

"Are these filters really necessary?" she teased.

"Hey, they came with the room," he defended, but he was smiling.

"Sure," she said, still giggling. "I'll bet you try out the glamour lens from time to time. Or perhaps the one that makes you look burlier."

Bryce frowned and pretended to be offended. He eyed the towel that was wrapped tightly around her slender figure. The bath cloth was tucked into itself, holding her breasts firmly in place. He moved to her side. One flick of his finger, and the towel fell to the floor. "Oops," he taunted.

"Don't you have somewhere to be?" she whispered, heart pounding.

He leaned in to kiss her exposed chest. "Not anywhere I can think of," he murmured as his lips roved over her breasts.

"I believe you said something about a flight to catch," she reminded him, but her arms were already wrapped around his neck and she tipped her head back to revel in his kisses.

"They can wait for me," he said. He was in no hurry to leave her behind.

Once Bryce was gone and Talia was alone, she dressed quickly, motivated by her desire to further explore the grounds. She wondered if one of the guards would have a key to the palace gardens. While putting on her shoes, she was startled by a knock on the door. Opening it, she was confronted by a lovely redheaded woman in her early fifties. While Talia had never met her in person, she recognized the woman as Bryce's mother, Grace, and gathered Bryce must have put his mother on the list of approved visitors.

Talia shyly invited her in, uncertain how Bryce's mother felt about the women that shared her son's bed. "You are quite lovely, dear," Grace told her. Talia thanked her, not sure what else to say.

"I can see what my son sees in you."

Talia looked down at her hands. "I am very fond of him," she confessed. "Your son is… very kind."

His mother smiled and asked, "Would you like to go shopping with me today?" Talia searched Grace's face for an ulterior motive, but all she saw was genuine kindness.

"I would love to," she said. "I'm ready to go now if you'd like."

Talia found the day with Bryce's mother a pleasant one. They shopped and went to lunch. Grace was genuine and down to earth, laughing and joking. During lunch, Grace brought up Kaden. "So, I hear that you ran into a little trouble with Kaden a while back."

Blushing, Talia nodded and self-consciously touched her cheek where the bruise was still faint. "I always knew that boy was trouble," Grace said. "But Bryce and he have been friends for so long…" she trailed off. "Sometimes there are things a woman can pick up on that the menfolk are blind to."

Talia nodded, but remained silent.

"So, tell me what you two have planned," Grace prodded. "Is Bryce going to have you stick around for a while?"

Talia was stunned by the queen's boldness, but not at all offended. "He asked me to stay indefinitely," she said, unsmiling.

"And what did you tell him?"

"I told him that I'd stay with him. I'd do anything for him." She looked off into the distance, her eyes misting.

"But you're worried. You don't want to see him give his heart to someone else. You love him." Grace's words were statements, not questions.

Talia nodded and felt a single tear streak down her face. "Silly, right?" She wiped the tear away, embarrassed at the raw display of emotion.

"Not at all." The queen offered a warm smile as she reached across the table to grab Talia's hand.

"I can see where Bryce gets his kind heart," Talia said. "I've never met anyone like him."

Grace smiled. "I am proud to see that his taste in women far exceeds his taste in friends."

Bryce stared out the window of his private jet. He smiled to himself, pleased at the outcome of his trip. His meetings with President Marcus Whitley and the advisory board for the Grand Americas had been fruitful. President Whitley's country had gone through a lot of change and rebirth since the Great World War of 2047. The United States, Canada, and Central America united into one country – now known as the Grand Americas. The merger had been met with some resistance from Alaska and Honduras, but eventually everything came together.

The president's historical knowledge and wisdom of what made the merger successful were invaluable to Bryce and his future plans for his kingdom. He wished he could share more with Talia. But it was both premature and dangerous to do so now. He would have to be patient. He sat back in his seat and closed his eyes, picturing Talia's smiling face. He was drifting off to sleep when a voice interrupted his slumber.

"Would you like to change before we land, sir?"

The prince looked down at his jeans, then up at his guard and smiled. "You know Jamison, my first order of business when I'm king will be to change the dress code. These jeans feel like butter on my skin. I wore them all through college. I miss them."

Jamison grinned. "You know, some people might say they're ugly as sin, sir. Not me of course. But some people."

"I would say those people have never worn these jeans," Bryce said, laughing as he stood to his feet to change.

CHAPTER 12

BY THE TIME BRYCE returned from his trip, Grace and Talia had both grown quite fond of one another. The queen enjoyed the company of someone with genuine interest in her, with no hidden agenda, and Talia felt the same. They'd spent countless hours together, tending to the palace gardens (where Talia was pleased to discover that she had quite the green thumb) and gossiping over long lunches.

"Your mother invited me to the dinner party tomorrow night," Talia told Bryce when they were finally alone.

"My mother?"

"Yes. We've been spending a great deal of time together these past several days. I really like her. She reminds me of you." Bryce smiled, pleased to be compared to his mother for once as opposed to his ruthless father. Talia really got him.

He mulled over the idea of her joining him for one of his mother's famous dinner engagements. He knew he didn't have to worry about whether she'd present herself properly (the slight bowing of her head to the gentlemen, curtsying to the ladies; offering her cheek only to those whom were her obvious elder), or if she selected the correct dinner fork. She would have been taught all such pleasantries and etiquette as part of the mandatory education program for Comforts. What he did have to worry about was her reaction if someone pissed her off. Talia's behavior at that point was anyone's guess. He smiled to himself. As much as he worried about it, it was one of the many things that made her so damn interesting. And appealing. Lord help him, he was in for an adventure when it came to this woman.

"You know, these dinner parties can be brutal," he said, clearing his throat. "If anyone finds out who you are, they may not be very kind to you."

Talia felt her face grow hot. "You're ashamed of me," she murmured and lowered her gaze.

"No, not at all. Talia, I just want to protect you and not subject you to those kinds of people."

She lifted her chin in defiance. "I can handle myself."

"I have no doubt you can. That's actually what kind of worries me. You have a tendency to say whatever pops into that pretty little head of yours. I need you to be on your best behavior. For me, okay?"

Talia promised him that she would, happy that he was agreeing to let her go. "There's just one more little problem," she said.

"What's that?"

"Well, if you think people will react better if they don't know who or what I am, I wonder how we're going to hide this." She lifted her arm, reminding Bryce of the tracking bracelet that imprisoned her wrist.

"Perhaps you can tell them I misbehaved, and you were forced to put me under house arrest."

Bryce examined her wrist, deep in thought. "I think I can remove that," he said.

"Get serious. We'd get into trouble."

"By whom? In case you've forgotten who my parents are..." he teased.

Talia shrugged her shoulders in agreement, realizing he was right. "Well, how do you propose we remove this thing?"

"Hmm... channel locks, a blow torch, perhaps."

"What?"

"I'm kidding. I know a jeweler here in town. He probably has a tool that I can borrow to remove it."

Within the hour the prince had secured a tool and was sitting cross-legged on the bed, facing Talia. With her wrist placed in his lap, he rotated the dial on the apparatus, watching as the small cutting tool severed the metal bracelet. His brow was furrowed in concentration. When the bracelet finally broke free, Talia rubbed her wrist, relieved to have it off.

Bryce lifted her bare wrist to his lips and kissed it. "Don't run away now," he teased.

CHAPTER 13

WHEN THEY ENTERED the party in the great dining hall, Bryce held Talia's hand casually in his, tracing the tiny bones in her wrist with his thumb. Talia wondered if Bryce even realized what he was doing – showing her this display of affection in public. Or maybe he didn't care what others thought. She hoped for the latter.

The décor of the dining hall was like something out of a fairy tale and it took Talia's breath away. Soft lights covered with white sheers tented the ceiling and draped to the floor. A crystal chandelier hung from the center of the room and was reflected on the black marble tile and in the many floor-length mirrors displayed around the room. Crystal vases holding black and red roses were used as centerpieces for the long dining table; a stark contrast to the white, linen tablecloths.

Talia surveyed the room, taking it all in. "This is amazing," she whispered in awe.

"You may change your mind once you've had a chance to mingle with our guests," Bryce said. The comment confused her, but she soon realized he was right to be concerned.

Talia tried to be on her best behavior, but the outlandish snobbery from the other guests soon wore on her. "Be good," Bryce whispered in her ear when he first saw evidence of her patience wearing thin. His tone was pleasant, but his words were a warning.

She flashed him a sweet smile, but inside she wanted to scream. When Grace first invited her to the party, she had been thrilled. She had often wondered what it would be like to run in the same circles as the high society ladies. But after spending some time with them, she realized how nasty many of the women could be.

When an announcement was made that dinner was ready, the men took their seats on one end of the long table, and the women on the other. Talia hoped to sit close to Grace, but instead found herself being seated amongst some of the younger ladies. The servants brought out massive trays loaded with lidded silver platters. A platter was set in front of each guest. The lids were lifted in unison and the aroma of wild boar and maple brine filled the dining room. It was all Talia could do not to lick her lips. She feigned patience, her hands folded in her lap, until the queen took her first bite.

Tradition considered it improper for anyone other than the host or hostess to be the first to sample the food. Historians believed the custom was originally established so the host could prove to the guests that the food being served wasn't poisoned. The concept seemed absurd but Inizi was steeped in its old-fashioned traditions.

A servant placed a napkin in the queen's lap. Grace thanked him, then reached for her fork. With remarkable poise she placed a dainty piece of meat on her fork and lifted it to her lips. She chewed, swallowed, then returned her fork to the table. "Please, dig in," she told her guests. Talia eagerly obliged.

As dinner unfolded, Talia's regard for the young ladies around her plummeted. They seemed crueler than most. Patience dangling by a thread, she did her best to ignore the gossiping women and concentrated on smiling and nodding while chewing her food slowly and tuning out any dialogue. But when Kaden's name came up in conversation, her ears pricked up.

"I hear that the prince got jealous that one of his little conquests was taking an interest in Kaden Huff, so he got mad and threw him out. Now Kaden isn't even allowed to enter the palace walls."

The anger bubbled up inside Talia until she could no longer contain it. She would not allow anyone to talk about Bryce that way, not when he had done so much for her. Without thinking, she picked up the glass of wine she'd been pretending to drink and threw it in the gossiping woman's face, silencing her lies and prompting stunned gasps from everyone else in the room.

From the opposite end of the table, Bryce wiped his mouth with his napkin, pushed back his chair, and stood to his feet. He politely excused himself for the evening, then strode over to where Talia had been sitting, taking her by the arm and leading her out of the banquet hall. Talia could hear the whispers in the room as she and Bryce made their exit.

"He's going to tan her backside," she heard one man say, and in addition to feeling humiliated, she shuddered to herself, fearing the man might be right.

When she and Bryce reached the hallway, Talia started in on her defense, but he cut her off. "We will discuss this in the privacy of my room," he told her. His eyes flashed with anger.

When they reached the prince's chambers, he crossed the room to his dresser and pulled out a nightgown for her. He thrust it into her arms and motioned her towards the bathroom. Talia opened her mouth to say something but quickly closed it, reconsidering. She took the nightgown and headed to the powder room to change, hoping that by her being accommodating, Bryce would offer up some forgiveness – though she knew she shouldn't hold out hope. Her actions were inexcusable, and she knew she deserved whatever was coming to her.

CHAPTER 14

WHEN TALIA ENTERED Bryce's bedchamber, her movements were slow and timid. Her flowing nightgown was thin, and she knew it would offer little protection from his wrath. Perhaps that's why he chose it. She had removed the pins from her hair and brushed it out, letting it dangle loosely at her narrow waist – precisely the way she knew he liked it. Her teeth were polished, and her face scrubbed free of makeup, apart from a subtle re-application of lip gloss.

Bryce stood glowering in the far corner of the room. He'd changed out of his evening clothes and into a pair of cotton blend trousers. He stood ramrod straight, shirtless, with his pants riding low on his hips. Talia would have found his appearance sexy if she wasn't so terrified. She bit her lower lip, tasting the faint pineapple flavor of her freshly applied gloss. Gripped by fear, she squared her shoulders and started to walk towards him, her legs wobbling.

"Bryce," she started, "I know you have to, um, punish me, but…" Her own voice was drowned out by the roaring in her ears. The room began to sway, and Talia found herself sinking to the floor.

Bryce closed the distance between them in two quick strides and caught Talia before she fell. He picked her up with minimal effort and laid her on his bed. He climbed into bed with her, wanting to comfort her, to hold her. He felt her entire body tremble as he stretched out beside her.

Talia mustered all the courage she had before turning towards him and speaking again. "I honestly know why you have to do what you have to do, but it scares me." She was being honest, but it wasn't so much the pain that frightened her. She knew that once Bryce hurt her it was going to change the way she felt about him, and that terrified her to her core.

Bryce pushed the hair back from her face to better study her expression. He knew he should take her over his knee for the stunt she pulled. According to society, it was his right. The use of corporal punishment on children had been done away with years ago, but with Comforts, it was still in common practice. According to the law Bryce could make Talia's flawless skin turn pink at the blows from his belt and be completely justified. But he also knew that he couldn't hurt her, and it was at that moment that he realized … he loved her. *God help him.*

Anger forgotten, he gathered her up in his arms. He felt her shiver and knew it wasn't just from the chill of the room. She was terrified of him, and the guilt washed over him because he realized a part of him had wanted to frighten her. He covered her with the thick quilt on the bed and rocked her in his arms. She buried her head in his chest, breaking down. Bryce was surprised at how fragile she seemed. She was usually so strong.

"Talia," he began. "Have I ever hurt you?"

She slowly lifted her head to look at him. He caressed her cheek with his thumb, wiping away her tears and waiting patiently for a reply. She wanted to remind him how bad it hurt when he sent her back to be with the other Comforts, but she shook her head *no* instead.

"And I would never, ever hurt you," he assured her. Her nightgown had slipped off her shoulder and he placed a tender kiss on her bare skin, just above her small tattoo, and waited for his words to sink in.

Talia's cries softened, and she snuggled closer to him. Her terror turned to relief, ensued by a deep longing for him. Bryce leaned in to kiss her and her body responded. She found herself trembling for an entirely different reason, racked with desire rather than fear.

"So, what did that woman say to get you so riled up?" he teased.

Talia didn't want to make him angry, but she also wanted to make it clear that she had been trying to stand up for him. She recapped what the woman had said, studying Bryce's reaction and expecting him to fly off the handle as she had.

Instead he chuckled. "Did you hit her with the red or the white?"

"Red," she said.

"Good girl," he laughed, wrapping his arms around her and kissing her again.

"Make love to me," she pleaded, and it was the only prompting Bryce needed.

He rose from the bed to undress. Talia's quivering fingers travelled to the waistband of his pants and she worked feverishly to push them past his hips. She remained perched on the edge of the bed as Bryce kicked the rest of the way out of his pants and stepped closer to her. To his surprise, Talia yanked down his undergarments and her mouth found his manhood. He groaned with pleasure, his head lulling backwards as his hands fisted in her hair. He was on the brink of losing control when Talia lifted her eyes to meet his, coaxing him back onto the bed.

Bryce crawled onto the bed beside her. She climbed onto his lap, straddling him. When his hands drifted beneath the thin folds of her nightgown, he expected to feel a barrier of lace panties, but was pleased to feel the nakedness of her buttocks instead.

He whispered his appreciation in her ear as he placed his hands on her bare skin, guiding her hips downwards and pushing himself deep inside her. Talia closed her eyes and tilted her head backwards. A smile played across her lips, and for the first time in as long as she could remember, she let down her guard and allowed herself to be completely free.

After they'd made love, Talia lay naked in Bryce's arms, her head resting on his bare chest. He was warm, and firm, and for the moment, completely hers.

"Is something the matter?" he asked in response to the silence that ensued.

"Oh nothing. I'm just sorry I'm so…" she began.

"What?"

"Damaged."

"We're all damaged," he told her, absentmindedly twisting the ends of her dark hair around his index finger.

"Yeah, but you shouldn't have to pay for his mistakes."

Bryce knew she meant Kaden, and he was silent as he mulled things over. What she didn't realize was how much he felt he deserved to pay for the wrongs done to her. He was responsible in ways she didn't yet know. Some day he would bolster the courage to tell her and let the chips fall where they may. But until then he would gladly stick around to pay the price, for as long as she would have him.

CHAPTER 15

WHEN TALIA AND BRYCE received an invitation from Grace the next morning, asking them to breakfast, they were both surprised. Talia was nervous about seeing the queen after making such a scene at the dinner party. But even more so, she was terrified about meeting Bryce's father for the first time. The king had been out of town during the dinner party, so she had yet to meet him in person.

"We don't have to go if you're not ready," Bryce told her.

"I'll be okay," Talia said. "And this time, I promise to be on my best behavior."

Bryce snorted in response, but then his expression turned grave. "Talia, I don't want to scare you, but you really have to be very well behaved. My father is not like my mother and me. He will not take lightly to any perceived disrespect, and he's the one person that I can't protect you from."

Talia shuddered, realizing the magnitude of the situation. "I promise that I will hold my tongue," she reassured him.

He stroked her hair and tucked a dark strand behind her ear. "Why do you stay with me?" he asked, taking her by surprise.

"Because I love you," she wanted to tell him. Instead she said, "Because you asked me to." The statement was equally true.

Bryce was quiet, contemplating her response. "Why did you ask me to stay?" she asked, unsettled by his silence. She met his gaze and thought he looked sad.

Struggling with an answer that wouldn't reveal too much, he finally responded, "Because I've never met anyone like you."

The full truth was that he needed her to stay. Talia made him feel powerful and vulnerable all at once. Loving her was easy. He only wished she felt the same. He could tell she desired him. She was a passionate woman. But he longed for her to love him, just as he loved her. Unrequited love was not a feeling he was used to.

Bryce held Talia's hand as they headed to his parents' personal dining area. He could tell she was nervous. Hell, he was nervous for her. She looked elegant. Her dark hair was curled and hung loosely down her back. He wanted to stay in bed and wind his fingers through her silky mane, but he knew an invitation to breakfast with his parents couldn't be ignored.

"What do I call your dad?" she asked before they reached the dining area.

"Oh. Hmm... good question. Sir, I guess."

"What do you call him?"

"When I *have* to talk to him, I usually call him *Sir*. Old habits. *Dad* on rare occasions."

Talia gathered Bryce wasn't close to his father. "What does your mother call him?"

"She calls him by his first name – Frankfurt. Sometimes just Frank."

Talia smiled. "I didn't even know that was his name."

"Well good grief, whatever you do, don't call him by his first name. My mother is probably the only one who can pull that off."

"I'll call him *your majesty*," she teased.

"That is probably a bit much," he laughed.

When they arrived at the dining area, Bryce's parents were already seated and sipping coffee. Grace rose from the table and hugged both Bryce and Talia, surprising them both for the second time that morning.

"I am so sorry about yesterday," Talia started to apologize.

"Oh, don't give it another thought. One of my dear friends was sitting close enough to hear the conversation. That gossiping nelly deserved what she got." Grace took Talia by the hand and leaned in closer. "I just hope my son wasn't too hard on you."

Talia blushed, remembering the way Bryce had tenderly made love to her when she had expected him to throttle her instead. "He was... understanding," she managed to say.

King Lachlan cleared his throat from his seat at the table, obviously summoning everyone to sit down. "Sir, I'd like you to meet Talia," Bryce said.

The king rose from the table. Talia resisted the urge to flee when she saw him up close. She offered a silent prayer of thanks that Bryce resembled his mother over his father. To her surprise, the king shook her hand and smiled. His thin skin stretched over hollow cheekbones made him look more like a skeleton than a living, breathing being, but Talia masked her fears and returned his firm handshake.

"I've been hearing a little palace buzz about you," the king told her with a wink. She smiled politely, then lowered her eyes and took a seat, wondering to herself what kind of talk he had heard. Bryce sat down beside her, draping an arm over her shoulders to settle her nerves.

When the food arrived, Talia welcomed the interruption. Waffles with strawberries and cream. Her favorite. As she took the first bite of her cream-saturated waffle, the king spoke. "So, what do you think of our home?"

"It's beautiful," Talia told him, after she'd swallowed her food and returned her fork to her plate. If there was one life lesson she remembered from her parents, it was to never speak with a mouthful of food. She dabbed her lips with her napkin and continued. "Bryce gave me a tour of the grounds and they are just so incredible."

"I see that you've taken to addressing my son pretty casually." The words were directed at Talia, but the king's look of disapproval was aimed at his son.

She started to apologize for her error, but Bryce cut in. "I have requested that she address me as such," he said coolly.

"Well, I guess if you don't care that your Comforts treat you with disrespect..."

Bryce slammed his napkin on the table. "Let's get something straight. My mutual respect for Talia, as well as my own male security, makes it possible for me to let her call me by my given name. And unlike you, I don't have Comforts in the plural."

Grace gasped and pressed her napkin to her mouth. Bryce felt instant regret at his choice of words, realizing his angry outburst served only to hurt his mother. "Mom, I'm sorry," he mumbled.

"Sir, I humbly apologize," Talia cut in, trying to defuse the situation. "I have the upmost regard for your son. I meant no disrespect and am happy to address you and your family in any way that you see fit." When Bryce started to argue, Talia squeezed his knee from beneath the table, silently pleading with him to end the argument.

"I've recently had the pleasure of introducing Talia to some of our local merchants," Grace chimed in.

"Oh, yes, some of the shops within the palace walls are so unique. I could window shop for hours. I especially liked the little store with the antique sports memorabilia," Talia said.

"I like that too," said King Lachlan. "I have an entire room decorated with sports memorabilia that I've collected over the years."

The tension lifting, Talia fell into casual conversation with Bryce's family. The king even shared a few humorous stories from Bryce's childhood, which had Talia laughing. When breakfast was over, King Lachlan kissed her hand and told her that it had been a pleasure to meet her. They said their goodbyes and Talia returned with Bryce to his room.

"You were amazing in there," Bryce said once they were finally alone. "I was so worried that you would lose your cool when instead it was me who nearly lost it."

"How does your mother handle your dad and all of his... women?"

"Obviously it bothers her. She loves my father, deeply. In his strange way, I guess he loves her too. But he's old-fashioned. He doesn't see it as cheating. He believes it's his right. You know, like concubines in biblical times almost."

"And what about you? What's your stance on having a Comfort, or Comforts, while you're married?"

"I think it's cheating. I would never do that to someone I was married to."

His words hit her like a direct blow to her heart. When he told her that he wanted her to stay, she thought he meant forever. Now she realized he only wanted her to stay until he found the woman he was supposed to marry.

"What's wrong?" Bryce asked, confused by her change in mood.

"Oh, nothing," she lied, forcing a smile.

Assuming he misread her, he changed the subject and offered to take her out on his boat for the afternoon. Talia tried to act excited, but inside she was dying as she pondered how long it would be before Bryce found someone else, and she was once again sent away to live with the other Comforts. She felt miserable, knowing when that day came, her heart would never recover.

CHAPTER 16

"YOU'RE DRESSED DIFFERENTLY today," Talia observed. She'd just stepped out of the shower and was toweling her hair. Bryce was sitting in a chair, reviewing his itinerary for the day. His trousers were a light-weight fabric and he was sporting a cotton-blend shirt rather than a button-up. His hair was tousled. "You look ... sexy," she admitted.

He smiled up at her. "Come sit with me," he invited, patting the chair beside him. Talia climbed into his lap instead.

"What's on the agenda today?" she asked.

"Today I'm traveling to some of the surrounding townships. My mother and I are doing some charity work." He looked proud without bragging.

"Wow, can I come?"

Bryce paused. "You wouldn't be bored?"

"Of course not."

"It could be dangerous. My family has enemies."

"Bryce, I really would like to go," she said patiently. She tried to keep her emotions out of the request. It confused her that he didn't seem to want her along.

"Then I'd be happy to have you join me," he told her. "But you can't go like this," he teased, slipping his hands beneath her robe and caressing her bare skin.

While she rushed to get ready, Bryce stepped into the hall to let his guards know Talia would be joining him. "I'll need both of you today," he said. "I won't take any chances with her."

Chad and Jamison both nodded.

"We'll be ready, sir," Jamison said.

When Bryce stepped back into the room, Talia met him at the door. "You really okay with me going?"

"I was being overprotective," he admitted. "Talia, I would love for you to come."

The first township was a success. The people formed long lines and Grace, Bryce, Talia, and a handful of volunteers distributed boxes filled with food, clothing, and bottled water. Each care package held a small sum of money, but the funds were carefully hidden. If word leaked out the boxes contained cash, it could put the volunteers in danger.

Bryce watched Talia as she handed out the goods to his subjects. Dressed in a simple, peach-colored dress she looked at ease, smiling and carrying on casual conversation with the townspeople. The people responded positively to her presence and Bryce was glad he agreed to let her come. He found it difficult to keep his eyes off her. She glanced up, sensing his gaze, and shot him a wink. He grinned and winked back.

"Oh, good grief, get it together," his mother teased him.

Bryce was successful at keeping his agenda from the press but invited one trusted journalist, Jason Tieg, to cover the occasion. The prince wanted a truthful, tasteful article that encouraged others to give back, put his family name in a positive light, but didn't exploit the poor or sensationalize the event. He'd utilized Jason in the past and had been impressed with his honest yet unbiased work.

On the road to the second township, their convoy was met with protestors. They lined the roadway. Bryce took Talia's hand in his. "Drive faster," he barked to the driver.

Talia heard Chad come across the radio in the car behind them. "They're sanctioned, sir."

The prince sighed with relief and gave Talia's hand a squeeze.

"What does he mean by *sanctioned*?" she asked.

"It means they have a permit for peaceful assembly. I think we'll be fine."

They reached the next township without further incident. The people were more standoffish than the previous villagers but took an instant liking to Talia. She moved through the crowds, convincing people to line up and accept the care packages. For those that remained afar off, she brought the packages to them. None refused her. Any resistance was squashed with her genuine smile and well-placed kind words.

"Take Talia back with you," Bryce told Jamison when they finished distributing the last of the care packages.

Talia gave him an inquisitive look.

"I have a little business to attend to," he told her. "I won't be long."

She stood on her tiptoes and kissed his cheek. "Okay, I'll see you back at your room."

When the convoy returned to the palace, minus Bryce and his lead guard, it was past dinner time. "Would you like to join me for dinner?" Grace invited Talia.

"I would love to."

The two women went to the main kitchen. Jamison trailed behind. Frances was by the stove, stirring a large kettle of soup. "Queen Grace," she said, setting down her ladle. "And sweet Talia," she gushed, walking around the kitchen island to offer Talia a hug.

"Hello, Frances," Talia said, beaming that she remembered her name.

"Where's Bry... Umm, where's the prince?" Frances asked. She cast an apologetic look in Grace's direction. She wasn't generally as informal with the queen.

"It will just be the three of us, Frances," Grace said, motioning for Jamison to join them. "We'll seat ourselves. Whatever you have in that kettle smells good."

Grace and Talia took their seats at one table and Jamison sat at another.

"Jamison, you can join us," Talia invited.

"That's okay, ma'am, I have a better view of our surroundings from here."

After they were seated, Talia complimented Grace on the design of the fireplace.

"Oh, Bryce told you." The queen looked flattered.

"He sure did."

"And I see he introduced you to the kitchen staff," Grace chuckled. "Bryce is so informal. It's sweet. I guess I'm more old-fashioned."

Talia smiled back at her. "You may not be on a first-name basis with all of the staff, but you have a kindness about you that everyone responds to."

"Thank you, but it pales in comparison to Bryce's charisma. He'll make a great king someday."

"Yes, he will," Talia agreed. She plastered a smile on her face and tried not to think about who Bryce's queen might be when that day came.

When dinner was over, Talia returned with Jamison to the prince's chambers. She noticed Chad sitting down the hall and realized Bryce was back. She knocked twice to announce her presence, then opened the door.

Bryce sat in the corner of the room. He held something small in his hands. "I thought you'd beat me back here," he said.

"Sorry, your mother and I had dinner."

"Oh what, I'm starving! I guess I'll have to find another dinner date," he teased.

"What's that?" Talia asked, pointing to the object in his hands.

He looked uncomfortable. "I got you a little something."

"You did?" She couldn't contain her excitement.

"It's not much," he warned.

101

"May I see it?" Talia took a seat next to him and held out her hand.

"I found the township where you used to live," he explained. "I tracked down the folks that let you stay with them for a while."

Talia sat on the edge of her chair. Her heart pounded in her chest.

Bryce did his best to hide the disdain he felt for the people he'd met. He would always judge them for giving Talia up. Then again, he supposed he should be grateful. Without them, he never would have met her.

"And?" she prodded.

"Oh, sorry, my mind drifted. Anyway, you might remember there was a box that your neighbors were able to save from the fire."

"Yes, that's right. It held a porcelain jewelry box that was my mother's. I was able to take one possession with me when I came to the palace, and that's what I chose." She smiled, but there was a deep sadness behind her eyes.

"Well, unfortunately, the family misplaced the box and most of the remaining contents. But they did find one thing." Bryce omitted the repulsive fact that the family demanded money for the small item they had managed to save. He ran his thumb over the artifact, then placed it in Talia's open palm.

She gasped. It was one of the chess pieces her father had hand-carved. The knight (though the intricate carving had smoothed out over the years). A tear rolled down her cheek and landed on the carved game piece. "I love it, Bryce," she whispered.

He rose from his chair and pulled her to her feet. "I really love it," she repeated. She threw her arms around his neck and hugged him tight. "Thank you."

He smiled to himself, pleased that she liked it. "You're welcome," he told her. It had taken some doing, but it was worth it to see how happy it made her.

Bryce was anxious to watch the coverage of the charity event, so he and Talia settled in to watch the evening news. He was pleased with the news story. There was footage of his mother and him, footage of the lines of townspeople (without focusing too much on their faces), and several close-up shots of Talia – smiling and passing out care packages. "You certainly captured the reporter's fancy," he teased, shutting off the television once the program was over.

Talia laughed. "I was in there quite a bit, wasn't I?"

Bryce grabbed a decorative candlestick and held it close to his mouth, feigning holding a microphone. Talking into it, he did his best impression of a news reporter. He sounded more like a deranged gameshow host. "Who is this mystery woman who has captured the hearts of the people and managed to tame the great Prince Lachlan, Inizi's most eligible bachelor?"

"Well, he's certainly not Inizi's most *humble* bachelor," Talia teased.

CHAPTER 17

WHEN TALIA AWOKE to find Bryce dressed, with several packed suitcases by the door, she froze. *Was Bryce going away again? Was he sending her back already?*

"Get dressed," he said cheerily. "We're going on a trip."

Her shoulders relaxed, and she smiled involuntarily. "Where are we going?"

"I thought you might like to come with me to see the Grand Americas."

She shot out of bed and scrambled to the dresser to find suitable clothing. "Really? I can come on your business trip?"

"No, this time isn't business, *ameerah*. We're going just for fun."

"I didn't know you knew how to just have fun," she teased.

"Should I remind you right now how much fun I can be?" Bryce crossed the room and took her in his arms. She squealed with delight when he dipped her backwards and pressed his lips to hers. "Now get dressed," he said, slapping her buttocks and planting another kiss on her cheek. "We leave in an hour."

Within the hour Talia found herself being whisked away on the royal family's private jet. She'd hoped she and Bryce could be alone, but she knew better than to expect it. With them was Jamison and another guard who wasn't as familiar.

"No Chadwick?" she asked.

"I gave him the day off. I think there might be a lady-friend in the picture."

Talia smiled to herself, wondering who Chadwick might be seeing in secret. "Good for him," she said.

She took a seat next to Bryce in the high-back reclining leather chair. A pretty flight attendant offered them fresh-squeezed orange juice and pastries. Bryce declined the pastries, but Talia took two. "And here I was feeling sorry for you, having to travel so much," she said.

"Hey, sometimes this seat hurts my back," he said, laughing and grabbing his lower back for theatrics.

Rolling her eyes, Talia bit into her first pastry. "Thanks for taking me with you," she said. She reached over and placed her hand in his.

He squeezed her hand and raised it to his lips. "The pleasure's all mine," he said. "Just wait until you see what I have in store for us."

Their first stop was the Big Island of Hawaii. Outside their hotel room, a warm rain began to fall, and Talia rummaged through her suitcase to find a bonnet to protect her head from the moisture. "What are these clothes?" she asked, as she took out each article of clothing and studied it closely. "These dresses are so… so short."

Bryce smiled as he watched her unpack and lay out each article on the bed. He'd asked one of his servants to buy clothes and pack, and as he watched what Talia was pulling out of the suitcase, he couldn't help but be pleased.

"You're in the Grand Americas now," he explained. "They don't feel the need to pretend we're living in another century. The people here dress for comfort."

"They hardly dress at all," Talia marveled, raising an eyebrow and looking skeptical as she stared at the pile of shorts and held the first sundress up to her body. It hit her legs somewhere around mid-thigh.

"That will look stunning on you," Bryce assured her.

She wasn't convinced, but she chose a blue sundress with lace overlay and headed toward the bathroom to grab a quick shower and get dressed before they headed to the beach.

When she stepped out of the bathroom, showered and ready, Bryce felt like his heart stopped. The sundress accentuated her tall, slender legs and the color matched her eyes. Damn if he didn't want to take her to bed and forget their outing. But he wanted to show her all that the Grand Americas had to offer – or as much as reasonably possible.

"What are you staring at?" she asked, feeling self-conscious and tugging at the hem of her dress. "It's too short, isn't it?"

He smiled and stepped towards her. "Talia, it's perfect." She smiled back at him and he pulled her in for a kiss. "You're perfect, *ameerah*."

No, you are, she thought, but she never spoke it.

As they walked hand-in-hand down the beach, Talia took everything in. The moon hovered over the water, casting a wistful glow, as the waves lapped along the shoreline. The landscape was beautiful, but having grown up on an island, she was anxious to get to the mainland. She kept the sentiment to herself, however. Bryce held her hand as they strolled side-by-side. He'd traded in his traditional attire for faded jeans, a T-shirt, and a ball cap. It was a look Talia adored. He looked comfortable, sexy, and completely at ease. The guards walked close behind but allowed some distance for privacy.

"How long are we here?" she asked.

"Here in Hawaii?"

"Hawaii. Away. Alone."

"I'm all yours for two weeks."

"Two weeks," she squealed, throwing her arms around his neck and planting a kiss on his cheek.

Bryce smiled. It had taken some elaborate rearranging to clear his schedule, but it had been necessary. He needed some time with Talia; needed some time away from it all. "Are you sure you can put up with me for that long?"

"I will do my best," she said.

The two weeks flew by in a whirlwind of excitement and romance. After spending a couple of days in Hawaii, Bryce took them to Mazatlán, Mexico, then the northern part of Arizona. The Grand Canyon remained, though it wasn't as grand as it once was. In the year 2035, some wealthy developers had convinced the desperate governor of the nearly-bankrupt state of Arizona that building condos along the red rock face of the canyon walls would be a great idea. The manmade structures marred the beautiful, natural landscape, though the glass walkways that connected the buildings were a spectacular design and far ahead of their time. During the Great World War, however, many of the walkways were severely damaged and had yet to be restored. Despite all this, Talia and Bryce spent hours exploring the area, taking it all in.

"Have you ever seen anything more beautiful?" Talia said breathlessly.

"No, never," Bryce said, although he was referring to her and not the scenery around her. He'd convinced her of the comfort of good ol' Grand Americas blue jeans and he was admiring the way the denim hugged her curves.

"You have no shame," she teased, once she realized he was gawking at her.

"I can't help myself," he growled with desire.

Talia's heart skipped as he drew her in closer to kiss her. She was pleased she didn't have to worry about who might witness their behavior – it didn't seem to matter away from Inizi. She fought to stop herself from telling him how much she loved him as she reveled in the rapture of his kiss.

Texas was the next destination of adventure. The state was massive – less inhabited since the war, but still vibrant and diverse. Talia begged Bryce to take her to the River Walk in San Antonia (not that he needed much convincing). He was pleased to find that he and Talia enjoyed many of the same things. As the couple passed one of the restaurants lining the waterfront, soft, instrumental music could be heard from the outside patio.

Bryce stopped and pulled Talia close. "Dance with me," he said.

He took her hand in his as his other hand slid down her waist. They danced under the soft light of the moon. A small crowd gathered to watch them as they moved in perfect rhythm to the music. Perhaps they recognized the prince. Perhaps they were hopeless romantics like Talia. Either way, Bryce didn't seem to notice the spectators, or care. He led her along with compassion and confidence. She moved in closer and rested her head on his shoulder as they swayed to the melody.

If Bryce didn't want to complicate things, he sure was making it difficult not to. When the song ended, and a fast-paced folk song began to play, Talia curtsied to the small crowd. The crowd applauded politely before moving on.

Further down the River Walk, a group of men approached with what appeared to be weapons in-hand. Their clothing was dingy, and Bryce presumed they were up to no good. He stepped protectively in front of Talia and the two guards flanked the young couple.

"Bryce," Talia started to say.

"It's okay, we've got this."

"Bryce," Talia said louder. She spoke with authority, not with concern.

He turned towards her, while keeping a watchful eye on the approaching men.

"They are not going to hurt us," she explained. "The items they carry are a symbolic gift. It's an old custom." She stepped around Bryce and his guards, then curtsied to the group. One by one the men presented her with the item they carried, and she bowed her head in gratitude and acceptance each time. Upon closer inspection, Bryce realized the items were crude, hand-carved statues. Talia turned and whispered to him, "Now you present them with something." Her tone hinted that *something* meant money.

When Bryce hesitated in the confusion, Jamison stepped forward and offered each man a gold coin. The currency was readily accepted in most regions. The men bowed, offered their thanks, then scurried down the path.

"Even the poor have their pride," Talia explained once the men were out of earshot. "Instead of asking for a handout, they seek a trade. Naturally, what the truly poor have to offer isn't of any interest to most – handmade tools, toys, or even shiny rocks – but it's a way for these people to feel like they are exchanging gifts with an equal versus receiving a handout from a stranger."

"How did I not know about this custom?" Bryce asked. "I spent the better part of four years in this country."

"It's not just a custom in this country. It was common in the township I grew up in as well." She blushed mildly as memories from her childhood bubbled to the surface; memories where she and her family offered their own homemade, paltry baubles in exchange for food or monies to make it through the tough times.

"Perhaps you didn't spend very much time around the, umm, less fortunate," she suggested.

"I must seem like a self-absorbed jerk to you," he said, half joking.

"No. We're just from different worlds." She smiled sweetly, but her words landed hard.

Back at the hotel Talia drifted in and out of sleep as she reflected on her day with Bryce. She worried the altercation on the River Walk would make him second guess their relationship; realize how very different they were. She felt instead that they complemented each other. Or at least that was her hope. She snuggled up closer to Bryce, who remained flat on his back, dead to the world. She tried to imagine life without him and felt a deep sadness wash over her.

"Bryce?" she whispered.

He stirred, then rolled on his side and spooned her body with his. "Talia," he whispered back. His sleepy, seductive tone made her quiver with delight. He had a way of expelling all her insecurities.

"Never mind," she said. She sighed a contented sigh and drifted back to sleep.

After Texas, the pair made a brief stop to see the Great Smoky Mountains that bordered North Carolina and Tennessee before Bryce whisked them away to New York City. When they landed in New York, it took Talia's breath away. Many internationally historic landmarks were destroyed in the last great war, but the Statue of Liberty was still standing. Lady Liberty stood tall and proud, her full lips and wideset eyes turned towards the sky. Much of New York had been rebuilt since the war, and now the architecture was a beautiful blend of old and new structures. Talia looked across the Hudson to watch a hawk fly low over the water, dipping the tips of its wings as it soared. Her eyes misted over as she took it all in.

With much of Inizi being uninhabited, Talia was amazed by the amount of people in the Grand Americas and the vast array of landscapes the country had to offer. There were sandy beaches, mountain ranges, deserts, and rugged forests.

"I never want to go home," she confessed.

Bryce smiled to himself. He very much felt the same. He'd attended college in the state of Oregon before the war, and he still felt homesick when he thought of his old dormitory. Before he'd met Talia, his plan had been to deny the throne and move back to the Grand Americas permanently. Now, instead of planning his escape, he found himself wanting to stay in Inizi and make it a better place – for Talia and for anyone in similar circumstances. It amazed him how quickly she'd changed everything for him, and how she had no idea what sort of impact she was making on his life.

"I do hope someday Inizi can be more like this," he said. "A land of opportunity where people can follow their dreams and build a life for themselves. Where there are options to escape a life of poverty." He glowed as he talked about his vision.

"If there's anyone that can make it happen, it would be you," Talia told him. She believed in him, and it made Bryce believe even more that someday it would be possible.

They were silent for much of the trip back. The jet included a private sleeping quarters and Bryce and Talia spent much of the flight lying in each other's arms. When they made love, it was soft and sweet. The trip had changed them both. They had tasted what life could be like as a regular couple without any social disparity between them. Bryce had been able to block out obligations and escape the shadow of his father.

"No regrets," Bryce finally said as he held her close.

"None at all," Talia said, turning to face him. "I know it'll be harder when we get back home. But I wouldn't trade this trip for anything."

Chadwick greeted the couple when they arrived back at Inizi. "Welcome back, sir. Talia."

Bryce nodded, but Talia offered Chadwick a quick hug. "Good to be back," she said, more for Bryce's benefit. She knew he was worried how they would both readjust to normal life. She wanted to assure him that, no matter the hardships, she wasn't going anywhere. At least, not while he wanted her around.

CHAPTER 18

WHEN THE MORNING SUN streamed through the windows, Talia groaned and put a pillow over her head. "Is someone feeling lazy today?" Bryce laughed.

"No," she said. "I feel sick. I swear the room is spinning."

The amused expression on Bryce's face evaporated and was replaced by concern. "You weren't feeling very well yesterday either."

"I know. I'm sorry. I'm no fun," Talia apologized, peeping at him from beneath the pillow and flashing him a sheepish grin.

He smiled and trailed his fingers over her thigh. "Oh, I think you're always fun," he teased. Talia started to laugh, but then shot out of bed and ran to the bathroom.

Hearing her retching from the other room, Bryce summoned his personal physician. When she emerged from the bathroom, Bryce was out of bed and throwing on some clothes. He tossed her a robe. "The doctor is on his way up."

She attempted to argue but he cut her off. "If you're coming down with something, I want it taken care of right away." Talia smiled to herself, amused that Bryce thought he could control the outcome of everything, even the flu.

When the doctor entered the room, Bryce excused himself, allowing Talia some privacy. At first, she found the doctor quite pleasant. Dressed in dark trousers and a white lab coat, the man introduced himself as Dr. Thomas, then took her temperature and asked her some routine questions. He patted her hand in reassurance. It was when he noticed her wrist that things changed. The doctor grabbed her by both hands, thrusting up the sleeves of her robe.

"Where is your bracelet?" he snapped.

"My... my bracelet?"

"Your bracelet," the doctor repeated. "The one you were issued right before your big reveal at the annual celebration."

Big reveal. Talia thought the term strangely inappropriate and she shuddered in memory of how helpless she had felt on that day. "I... I removed it," she told him. "The prince trusts me. He didn't feel there was a need for anyone to track me."

"That wasn't just a tracking device. That also served as your time-released birth control. The medication was absorbed through your skin and entered your bloodstream," the doctor seethed. "But then again, you probably already knew that, didn't you?"

Talia was fuming at the allegation, but more than that, she was terrified at what the doctor's accusations were suggesting. "You think I might be pregnant?" she asked, choking back tears.

"Well, we'll soon find out." Dr. Thomas reached into his bag and pulled out a small, hand-held gadget. After prepping the strange instrument, he motioned to Talia to put her finger on what appeared to be a small scanner located in the middle of the device.

With a trembling hand, she placed her index finger on the scanner. She felt the prick of a needle and watched the dials on the little machine start to spin. When the results flashed across the screen, she promptly took a seat, worried her legs would not hold her.

"Well, you are pregnant," he spoke sharply. Talia could tell he was furious. He was practically spitting the words out at her. "Your little plan isn't going to work, you know. Do you think you're the first little harlot to try and entrap...?"

"That is quite enough!" Bryce's voice boomed from the doorway. His presence startled Talia but didn't have near the effect on her that it did on Dr. Thomas – who nearly jumped out of his own skin, then scurried from the room, leaving his bag of medical instruments behind. Talia remained in her seat, unable to move as Bryce approached her.

"I didn't, you know." Her voice was soft, but firm. Tears stung her eyes, but she willed them not to spill over while she suppressed the urge to flee.

"Didn't what?" Bryce asked. His tone sounded strange to her, almost as if he was amused.

"I didn't do this on purpose," she said, shrinking back into her chair.

"I never thought for a moment that you did." He calmly took a seat across from her.

Talia's thoughts were in turmoil as she rifled through her brain for a solution. She had no intention of giving up her baby. It was a part of her, but more importantly, it was a part of Bryce, the man she loved more than anything – and perhaps the only part of him she had any hope of keeping.

"I think it's kind of sexy," he finally spoke, interrupting her tormented thoughts. She glanced over at him, confused. His expression was one of triumph.

"What's sexy?" she asked, curious where this line of dialogue was heading, but no longer frightened of his reaction.

"My beautiful Talia, carrying my baby." She loved the way he emphasized the word *my*. Overcome with emotion and relief, she felt the tears begin to fall. She stood from her chair and took a seat in Bryce's lap. He hooked an arm around her waist and playfully patted her belly.

"I thought you'd be angry," she admitted.

"I must admit, I am surprised. But I'm not angry. Why would I be angry? If memory serves correctly, it took both of us to get into this little, uh, predicament."

Talia's cheeks reddened, and she rested her head against Bryce's chest to avoid his stare.

"I guess in hindsight I should have looked more into what that bracelet was for before so nicely helping you remove it," he teased. He kissed the top of her head and held her tighter.

She laughed and nestled into his warmth. "I agree. In fact, I may blame you for this entirely."

They both knew keeping the baby would result in a host of problems that would soon need addressed, but for now they chose to be happy.

Bryce summoned Dr. Thomas back to his chambers. Talia left the room to take a shower, not wanting to face the unpleasant doctor and his accusing stare. The doctor was humbled when he returned and apologized profusely to the prince for his earlier behavior.

"Save it," Bryce told him. "You are here to collect your things, but I also want to make something bloody clear. You will not speak of this to anyone, is that understood?" The doctor gave his word, and once Bryce was convinced the promise was genuine, he dismissed him from the room.

After the doctor left, Bryce wandered to the bathroom to check on Talia. He found her standing naked in front of the sink, wet hair dripping down her back. Her right hand protectively covered her abdomen as she stared at her reflection in the mirror.

Bryce was fascinated by the notion of Talia's firm belly becoming swollen with his child. He paused in the doorway to watch her. Finally noticing his presence, she dropped her hand to her side and turned to face him, embarrassed.

"You're so beautiful," he murmured. He stepped into the bathroom and pulled her into his arms, kissing her as his hands explored her naked body.

Talia tugged at his shirt, feverishly returning his kisses. "Make love to me," she begged.

"I fully intend to." He gathered her in his arms and headed towards the bed.

CHAPTER 19

WITH BRYCE ONCE AGAIN away on business, Talia decided to take advantage of her free time and get to know Grace better. She only hoped that Grace would have time for her.

She had barely opened the bedroom door when a voice interrupted her thoughts. "Going somewhere, Miss?"

She rolled her eyes at the guard's tenacity. "Chadwick…"

"Please, call me Chad."

"I will once you start calling me Talia instead of *Miss*."

"That's fair," Chadwick agreed. "Now, where shall I escort you to, *Talia*?"

"Actually, *Chad*, I was hoping to see if Grace, err, the queen, was interested in doing something today."

"Oh, she and King Lachlan left for Paris this morning. Anniversary trip."

Talia was disappointed. "Oh, I see." She thought she could perhaps go back to visit the Comforts but seeing them reminded her of who she was and that someday Bryce would be done with her.

Chadwick could tell Talia was disheartened. More than that, she seemed sad. He had become fond of her and didn't like to see her upset. "Hey, you and I can hang out today," he offered.

"Really?" Talia was surprised, but the offer piqued her interest.

"Of course. I am, after all, assigned to protect you. We might as well have some fun." The guard was grinning like a school boy. It was the first time Talia had seen him so relaxed. "Do you want to go visit your friends again?" he asked.

When she told him "no," she thought she witnessed a flicker of disappointment. The reaction puzzled her. Perhaps she'd imagined it. "What are your feelings on ice cream for breakfast?" she asked. Oddly enough, it was one of the few things her sensitive stomach could handle in the mornings.

"Sounds great. Would you like some pickles with that?"

Talia felt herself flush. "So, um, I guess that means you know then?"

"I've served under Bryce for a long time. There are some things he shares in confidence, especially when he's excited about something."

"So, he really is excited?" She secretly feared Bryce may have exaggerated his enthusiasm about the baby.

"I've never seen him happier," Chadwick admitted honestly, marveling at how Talia's eyes lit up at his words. By his observations, she really had no idea how much the prince cared about her.

By the time they reached the ice cream parlor, Talia was chattering about baby names. She hadn't realized until now just how much she missed having someone other than Bryce to confide in. She hadn't even dared to tell Grace about the baby, fearing that word would get back to the king.

After they had polished off their waffle cones, Talia asked Chadwick if he would escort her to some of the local shops. "I love to window shop," she said.

"You'll be doing more than window shopping today," he informed her. "Bryce left instructions to let you purchase anything you desired. Obviously, he has in-store credit wherever you'd like."

"Normally I'd argue about spending his money," she said, "but today I'm in a shopping mood, so Bryce may regret those instructions."

After a couple hours of shopping, and loaded down with packages, Chadwick escorted Talia back to Bryce's chambers. "I had a lovely time, Chadwi…err, Chad," she told him. She gave him a quick kiss on the cheek before taking the shopping bags from him. She entered the room and closed the door behind her.

After setting down her packages, she started to undress, wanting to slip into something more comfortable. Although her body hadn't changed enough to be obvious to anyone else, she herself could feel her clothes becoming more constrictive. No sooner had her dress hit the floor, she heard a rustling from the hallway by the bathroom. She smiled, figuring Bryce must have returned early from his trip to surprise her. She crept towards the bathroom, tiptoeing barefoot in nothing more than her full slip.

Before she reached the bathroom door, a tall figure darkened the doorway and Talia froze. It wasn't Bryce. It was Kaden. She leapt backwards but wasn't quick enough to avoid his advances. He grabbed her by the front of her slip, pulling her towards him.

"I've been waiting for the moment to catch you alone." His breathing was erratic, and his breath smelled of booze.

"How did you get in here?" she asked, her voice barely a whisper.

"Easy. Your room was left unguarded. Looks like you were too busy flirting around with Chadwick. I wonder, does Bryce know how friendly you are with his guard?"

Talia glared at him, desperate to formulate a plan. She was frightened – not only for herself, but for her baby. "Kaden, please, you should leave now before someone sees you here. They will lock you up. If you leave now, I promise I won't tell anyone that you were here."

"Nice try, Talia. You've always been an awful liar." Kaden clamped his lips down on hers. She twisted herself free and ran down the hallway towards the main bedroom. Racing to the dresser, she opened the top drawer and retrieved Bryce's hunting knife from beneath a neat layer of socks.

She turned around in time to face him. "Back off," she warned. "I am prepared to use this."

Kaden scoffed, but paused for a moment. "You don't really expect me to believe that you're going to use that, do you?" He took another step toward her.

"Please. I'm begging you." Her voice cracked, and the knife shook in her hands.

Unconvinced he was in any real danger, Kaden rushed at Talia, knocking her to the floor and sending the knife sliding across the bedroom floor. Her head hit the floor, temporarily disorienting her, but she quickly recovered. She kicked with all her might, her foot connecting with his temple.

While he was left reeling from the blow, Talia crawled to the knife. When Kaden grabbed her by the hair, she swung around and plunged the knife blindly in his direction. She was sickened when she felt it sink into his torso. As the blood started to seep through his clothing, she withdrew the knife and began to scream.

Hearing her cries, Chadwick bolted through the bedroom door and found Talia and Kaden in a heap on the floor. Kaden was bleeding profusely, and Talia was crying, her hands covered in blood. Seeing her torn underskirt, Chadwick worried he might be too late. Talia still clung to the knife. Chadwick sunk to his knees in front of her, closing his fingers over her wrist and coaxing her to release the knife.

She dropped her hold on the weapon, then buried her head in Chadwick's chest. "Did he hurt you?" he asked. She shook her head *no* but couldn't stop herself from crying.

Chadwick could tell Kaden was losing consciousness, so he crossed the floor to the touchscreen apparatus and summoned a doctor. Knowing he didn't have much time, he took some clothes from the dresser and used them as a compress to control the bleeding. "Listen carefully," he told Talia. "I need you to get dressed and leave this room immediately."

"What? Why?" Talia was failing to make sense of Chadwick's demands.

"You are a Comfort. Although somewhat disgraced, Kaden is still considered a nobleman. The law strictly states that any attack on a nobleman by a Comfort is punishable by death. You can claim self-defense, but it will be your word against his. You need to get out of here, quickly."

When she started to argue, Chadwick practically screamed at her. "Talia, you need to get out of here, now!"

She ran to the bathroom to wash the blood from her hands and smooth her hair. She threw on her dress from where it lay in a heap on the bedroom floor, then fled from the room, casting one final glance in Chadwick's direction.

CHAPTER 20

TALIA SPENT THE NEXT couple of hours roaming the palace grounds to establish her alibi. She made a few purchases and had a light meal at one of the local cafés. All the while she worried about Chadwick and what he might be going through to cover for her. She also worried about Kaden. As much as she hated him, she didn't want to be responsible for his death. The thought sickened her. After what seemed like an eternity, she returned to her bedroom to find it surrounded by guards.

"What's going on here?" she asked, hoping she sounded convincing.

One of the guards explained that Kaden had broken into the room in an attempt to harm Bryce. When Chadwick found him while performing a routine sweep of the room, Kaden attacked him, and he was forced to defend himself with a knife.

"That's awful," Talia said. "Is Chadwick okay?"

"Yes," the guard reassured her. "He is filing an official report. The prince is on a plane back here to review the report."

Talia was relieved that Bryce was returning. "And Kaden? How is he?" She could barely get the words out, fearful of the answer.

"He's in surgery right now, but he's expected to pull through." Despite her hatred for Kaden, the news was a relief. She didn't think her conscience could handle if she'd taken another person's life.

Once the guards were satisfied with Chadwick's version of the events, they dispersed, except for two guards who were selected to personally guard Talia until Bryce returned. A brief time later the cleaning staff arrived to tidy up the room and remove any evidence of the struggle.

When Talia heard a knock on the door, she hurried towards it, hoping it would be Bryce. Instead, Chadwick appeared, looking a little tired. When he entered the room, she flung her arms around his neck and once again kissed his cheek to thank him for all he had done.

"I am so sorry you had to lie for me," she said.

"I'd do it again in a heartbeat."

"Ahem." Bryce cleared his throat from the doorway. Neither Talia nor Chadwick had heard him enter the room.

"Does one of you care to explain exactly what the hell is going on here?" Bryce was angry, something that surprised Talia. But then she realized he had no idea what happened, only the version of the story Chadwick had shared with everyone.

She was about to explain when Chadwick interrupted her. "Talia was just thanking me for protecting you from Kaden, sir." To Talia's surprise, Chadwick was sticking to the same story he told everyone else.

"Is that so?" Bryce asked, sounding skeptical. Talia couldn't be sure, but it looked like he was glaring in her direction.

"Yes, yes sir it is," Chadwick reaffirmed.

"Well, I do appreciate that you found him," Bryce said. "But I did give you specific instructions not to let Talia out of your sight. I would like to know what she was doing roaming around the palace grounds without you."

Outraged by Bryce's reaction, Talia leapt to Chadwick's defense. "Bryce, Chad should be thanked for his heroism today, not chastised!"

Bryce made a mental note of the way Talia referred to his guard. "You are right, Talia. Chadwick, I would like to thank you for your service today. I will make sure you are well compensated. Now if you will both excuse me, I have some business matters to attend to." His words were clipped, his voice flat. With that, he walked away.

Talia was visibly shaken by Bryce's behavior. "Maybe we should have just told him the truth, Chad."

Shaking his head, Chadwick moved closer to her and placed his hands on her shoulders to calm her. "It's alright. He'll cool down. That's the first time I've ever lied to him."

"Why did you?"

Chadwick lifted Talia's chin, locking his eyes on hers. "Bryce assigned me to protect you. That's what I'm going to do, even if it's from him."

"What do you mean? Bryce would never tell anyone that I was the one who stabbed Kaden. Would he?"

The guard was silent as he contemplated the question. "I'm just not sure. I am reasonably certain that he wouldn't, but his father is the very king who set the current laws in place. Not to mention that Kaden and Bryce were lifelong friends. I couldn't take that chance."

"I think it was an unnecessary precaution, but I am very grateful to you. Thank you, Chad."

When Bryce returned to his room later that evening, Talia nervously awaited him. She was prepared for an argument, but Bryce didn't say anything, which was somehow more disconcerting.

They got ready for bed in silence. When Bryce stretched out in bed beside her, Talia could tell that he was restless. His heavy breathing gave him away. "What's wrong?" she finally asked.

"Why did you kiss Chadwick?" The question was out before Bryce could rein it back in.

"I kissed him on the cheek."

"I know. But why? Were you trying to seduce him?" His voice was strained. Talia wanted to be angry, but she could hear the hurt in his words.

She sat up in bed, switching on the lamp on the nightstand. "Bryce, I care about Chad as a friend. Why would you ever think I would try to seduce him?"

Wincing at the casual way she once again referred to his personal guard, Bryce answered, "You seduced me once." His words were clipped, bitter. "It wouldn't be the first time you used your beauty to get something you wanted."

This time it was Talia's turn to be angry. "Is that what you think? That I seduced you for some personal gain? And why would I do that? So

I wouldn't have to go back to being with the other Comforts?" Her cheeks burned in anger and humiliation.

"Didn't you?" He sounded so callous Talia felt as if she'd been punched in the gut.

"And I suppose I also got pregnant just to trap you?" she hissed.

"If the baby is even mine." Bryce knew he was going too far, but he had witnessed the embrace between Talia and Chadwick and he refused to be the fool.

"I don't know where all of this is coming from, but you are not the man I thought you were. How dare you treat me like some sort of a harlot because I dared to care about you! I want nothing more to do with you. I would like to go back to my room now."

Bryce knew he should stop her, but jealous rage clouded his judgment. "I will have Chadwick escort you. I'm sure you will like that."

"Yes, yes I think I would." Talia refused to cry. There would be plenty of time for that once she'd reached her modest living quarters.

Moments later Chadwick was standing in the bedroom doorway. He and Bryce did not exchange a single word. When Talia's suitcase was packed, Chadwick took it from her and held open the bedroom door as she made her exit, head held high.

"What happened?" he asked once he was certain he and Talia were out of earshot.

Unable to stop herself, she broke down. "He practically accused me of sleeping with you. He even suggested the baby isn't his."

Chadwick's jaw tightened. In all his years of service under Bryce, Chadwick had never spoken a word against him, but he had also never seen the prince act so nasty, especially towards a woman. "I am sure he didn't mean it," was all he could manage without revealing his own anger.

"Oh Chad, what should I do? A pregnant Comfort!" Talia was near hysterics.

"Don't worry. I will take care of it. Trust me. Everything will be better in the morning, I promise."

Talia was doubtful, but she did manage to stop weeping. She followed behind Chadwick in silence as he led her down several corridors. When they arrived outside of a large doorway within the palace, she looked confused. "This isn't the way to my living quarters."

"I know. There's no way I am sending you back there. This is one of the palace guest suites. You will sleep here tonight. Don't let anyone else in. I will be back for you in the morning."

A tear trickled down her face. Unable to stop himself, Chadwick reached over and wiped it away. "Everything's going to be okay. I promise." He gave her hair a reassuring tug, then walked away, leaving Talia alone and heartbroken.

CHAPTER 21

BRYCE WAS SITTING in his room, brooding, when he was interrupted by a knock at the door. Opening it, he found Chadwick standing in the doorway looking equally cross.

"You've got a lot of nerve," Bryce told him.

Ignoring him, Chadwick entered the room without being invited and closed the door behind him. He wanted to be sure there weren't any witnesses to what he was about to say.

"In all of the years that I have known you, I have never seen you treat another living soul as cruelly as you just treated Talia. And if there was ever someone who didn't deserve it, it would be her." His voice shook – mildly in fear of the consequences of his insubordination, but mostly with rage.

"Oh, I'm sorry. Did I hurt your girlfriend's feelings?" Bryce knew he was being childish. After all, it wasn't Talia's fault if she didn't care for him as much as he did for her. She had done what she needed to do to survive.

Drawing an arduous breath, Chadwick asked, "May I speak frankly?"

"By all means." Bryce threw his arms in the air, impatient and unamused. But he started to soften as Chadwick filled him in on the actual events of the evening. Once Bryce learned that it was Talia who had stabbed Kaden, he sunk into a chair in the corner of the room.

"And why didn't she tell me this earlier?"

"I advised her not to, sir," Chadwick said. He struggled to realign his emotions and subjection. "I was worried that you would feel obligated to your friend – or somehow feel obligated to uphold your father's law."

"The one that makes it a capital crime for a Comfort to attack a nobleman," Bryce said, starting to understand.

"Correct. In Talia's defense, she told me she thought my fears weren't warranted. She assured me you wouldn't do anything to hurt her." Chadwick's voice trailed off and Bryce understood why. His actions had probably hurt Talia more than anyone had expected.

All the anger that the prince had been feeling he turned on himself. "I really screwed up Chad. I don't think that I can ever thank you enough for what you did for her – for us."

Chadwick looked embarrassed at Bryce's praise. "Sir, if you don't mind me saying so, there's probably someone else you should be apologizing to."

Bryce nodded in agreement. "Where did you stash her?"

"Sir?"

"Oh, come on Chad. You and I both know you wouldn't have sent her back to be with the other Comforts. It is, after all, one of the reasons I entrusted her to you."

The guard grinned. "I moved her to the guest suite in the east wing," he admitted.

Talia was brushing her teeth before bed when she heard a knock at the door of her suite. Heeding Chadwick's stern warning to not let anyone else in but him, she crept to the door and stood on her tiptoes to look out the tiny peephole. When she saw Bryce outside the door, she nearly toppled backwards.

After composing herself, she answered the door. Bryce could see that she was angry, and he hoped she could forgive him. "Chadwick told me what really happened," he managed to say, ducking under her arm to enter her room.

Talia shut the door behind them. "So, are you here to arrest me?" Her eyes were swollen from crying, and she looked pale, but to Bryce she'd never looked more beautiful.

He slowly approached her, searching her face to assess how she was handling herself. She backed away from him, an involuntary whimper escaping her lips. *Please don't hurt me*, she pleaded in her head. He could make out the fear in her eyes, surfacing above the anger, and he stopped in his tracks, hating himself for the damage he'd done and the trust he knew he'd broken.

"No, *ameerah*. I came back to make sure you were okay."

"He didn't hurt me," she said. *Not like you did.*

"And our baby?"

"I did hit the floor in the struggle, but I'm sure the baby's fine."

Bryce had never felt such self-loathing. "All the same, I'm going to have a doctor check you out." He expected her to argue, but she remained silent.

"Talia, I can't even begin to tell you how sorry I am," he continued. "When I saw you and Chadwick together, I just went crazy."

"I was only thanking him for saving me."

"I know that now. But even if it had been more than that, I shouldn't have reacted that way."

"What you said about me trying to seduce you…" she began.

"Don't. You don't have to explain yourself. I was being an idiot."

"But I want to. I will admit at first that was my plan, but I want you to know that I gave myself to you because I wanted you. I did so because I love you."

The tears streamed down Talia's cheeks and Bryce melted. He had been so sure she didn't care for him at all like he cared for her.

"Talia, I am so sorry. I had no idea you felt that way about me. When I once asked you why you stayed with me, you only said that it was because I had asked you to."

"Because you told me you didn't want to complicate things," she said, the pitch of her voice rising. She wiped her eyes with the back of her hand. "I was afraid if I told you, that you'd send me back. But this doesn't have to complicate things," she continued. "When the time comes for you to take a wife, I won't stand in your way."

Bryce looked confused. "What makes you think I'd ever choose anyone else but you?"

"You told me that you'd never have a Comfort while you were married," she reminded him.

"That is true, I wouldn't. But I have no intention of being with anyone else but you."

"If you think you have to stay with me for the baby..."

"I am not staying for the baby," he interrupted. "Talia, I love you. I thought by now it was obvious."

"You... you do?"

"Of course I do. I don't know at what point that I fell in love with you. Maybe it was from the moment you walked onto that stage and attempted to hurl a vase into the crowd. All I know is that I love you."

Talia stood in stunned silence.

Bryce pulled her into his arms, breathing her in. "Oh Talia," he told her. "My beautiful Talia. I don't deserve you, but I love you. And even if I can never marry you, I never want to be with anyone else. Please, please stay with me. Not just because I asked you to, but because you want to."

"I do want to," she told him. "And I will. I love you too. More than anything."

Pulling her even closer, Bryce brushed his lips over hers. "I am so sorry for what I put you through and that I wasn't there for you."

"Bryce, you can't protect me all of the time. Besides, I can handle myself."

"Clearly," he chuckled, despite the circumstances.

He felt Talia stiffen in his arms. "Bryce, what do we do when Kaden wakes up from surgery? What if he tells people it was me who stabbed him? I could be brought up on charges."

Bryce silenced her words with another kiss. Her eyes were wide, fearful. "I will take care of everything," he assured her. "Kaden will be in a bigger world of trouble if he admits he also attacked you. I will convince him to go along with Chadwick's story in exchange for a lighter sentence. I don't want you to worry about anything. I'm going to call the doctor to come up here now, just to get a look at you and the baby."

Talia detested the thought of seeing the vile doctor again, but her disdain for the man was not as strong as her concern for her unborn baby, so she nodded her head in agreement.

When Dr. Thomas entered the guest suite, he appeared nervous. "Sir, I assure you that I have not told anyone about the baby," he began when Bryce let him in.

"That's not why I called you here, doctor. Talia had a little fall today and I want you to take a look at her and make sure that everything is alright."

The doctor looked relieved. He crossed the room to where Talia was resting on the sofa and asked, "How are you feeling?" His demeanor was pleasant, and Talia observed that when he wasn't being such a jerk, he had a great bedside manner.

"I feel fine. Bryce just worries," she said. She noticed the faint look of disapproval that passed over the doctor's face at the informal way she addressed the prince and made a mental note to ask Bryce what she should call him when other people were around.

The doctor took Talia's blood pressure, listened to her breathing, and produced a small device from his bag and placed it on her bare stomach. "To check the baby's heartbeat," he explained, smiling, and Talia returned a nervous smile.

Bryce grasped her hand, and both held their breath as they waited to hear the faint beating of their baby's heart, an indicator that everything was fine. They both sighed with relief and happiness when they heard the faint sound.

"Everything sounds good," Dr. Thomas said, but I'd also like to do a quick scan to be certain. Bryce nodded, but the doctor cleared his throat nervously. "I don't have the equipment with me. I'll need to go get it."

The prince nodded in approval.

Dr. Thomas returned moments later, a tablet in one hand and a small, egg-shaped device in the other. Talia recognized the instrument from the days she had assisted her mother at the hospital. It had revolutionized imaging in the medical profession, rendering ultrasounds and CT scans obsolete.

After she nodded her permission, the doctor propped the tablet on the coffee table, then placed the smooth, oval device on her bare abdomen. The image appeared on the screen in an instant. The doctor adjusted a small dial and the image came into focus. Talia and Bryce couldn't quite make out everything they were seeing, but recognized the shape of their tiny, growing baby.

"Everything looks perfect," the doctor said after a few minutes, switching off the machine.

Bryce was so grateful that he hugged him. "Thank you, Dr. Thomas," he said, stepping back and clearing his throat in embarrassment. "I won't forget your help, or your discretion," he said in earnest as he saw the doctor out.

CHAPTER 22

AFTER HE HAD MOVED Talia back into his room and saw to it that she was settled, Bryce went to see Kaden at the hospital. "He's out of surgery and resting comfortably," the surgeon told him. "He's heavily sedated, so I'm afraid you won't be able to speak to him for a little while yet."

"I'll wait out here. When he's awake, I want to be the first to know," Bryce demanded.

He took a seat in the hallway and asked an orderly to bring him a fresh cup of coffee. "Please," he added, picturing Talia scolding him for forgetting his manners. He smiled to himself. It was cliché, but she made him a better man.

When he received the news that Kaden was awake, Bryce didn't waste any time getting to his room. He ordered all the hospital staff out and shut the door to be sure no one was around to hear their conversation.

"Looks like you got yourself a fighter on your hands. I'd watch my back when I went to sleep if I were you," Kaden said. Even in a groggy state, his cruelty was evident, and Bryce wondered how Kaden had managed to keep it hidden for so many years. Then again, perhaps Bryce had been blind to it.

"Cut the bull," he said. "This is what is going to happen. I will ensure the courts cut you a deal in exchange for you going along with a different set of events than what may or may not have transpired."

"And what do I get out of this so-called deal?"

"You get to live. Isn't that enough?" Bryce roared. He leaned down, face inches from Kaden's.

"Smacking around some Comfort isn't a capital offense. The courts would never even come close to the death penalty."

Bryce lost his cool. He grabbed Kaden by the throat and squeezed. "I wasn't referring to how the courts would handle it," he said through his teeth, and Kaden had enough sense about him to know that his childhood friend wasn't bluffing.

When Bryce released his hold, Kaden looked less smug. "What did you have in mind?" he asked. His voice was hoarse.

"You will be sentenced to three months of imprisonment, after which time you will leave the palace grounds. You will move to one of the outer townships and learn to make a living without the help of me or my family."

"I'll tell any story you want me to tell," Kaden said. "A little prison time is worth getting to taste that sweet flower of yours."

Bryce felt sick. "She said you didn't do anything." His voice faltered, and he prayed Kaden was lying.

"Aww, and you believed her. That's sweet. Did she also tell you there's nothing going on with her and your personal guard? Tsk...tsk... such naivety."

"That's quite enough," Bryce interrupted, slamming his fist down on the hospital tray positioned by the bed. He knew in his heart that everything out of Kaden's mouth was a lie, but the words still sickened him.

"What's the matter? The truth too painful for you?"

"Do we have a deal or not?"

"Looks like I don't have much choice," Kaden said without enthusiasm.

"Good. You don't." Bryce tossed a copy of Chadwick's statement at him. "Read this. Memorize it. I will send someone up here shortly to take your confession. Your accounts had better match up with Chadwick's."

As Bryce turned to leave the room, Kaden spoke up. "Tell me something, how did Talia react when you told her that you were the one who got me the job looking after the Comforts?"

Bryce stopped in his tracks. He felt the hairs on his neck stand on end. "Oh, you never told her," Kaden continued, shaking his head. "That's quite the predicament you've gotten yourself into."

"Talia would understand," Bryce lied, unable to turn around and look Kaden in the eye.

"Hmm, if you say so, mate."

Bryce had no response. He knew Kaden was probably right.

After convincing Kaden to take a plea deal in exchange for his cooperation (aka, going along with Chadwick's fictional story), Bryce returned to his room. Talia was awake and wringing her hands, waiting for news of how it went.

"Well?" she asked.

"Kaden has agreed to keep your story." Bryce seemed different than he had been when he left to talk to Kaden. His mood was dark.

"What is it that's bothering you?" Talia asked, taking a seat on the edge of the bed.

He sat down beside her and turned to face her. "It was just something Kaden said." He paused and took a deep, deliberate breath. "Talia, I want you to know, no matter what happened, it's okay. It's not your fault."

She cocked her head to the side, confused. Bryce continued. "You know if Kaden did something to you, and you're afraid to tell me, nothing you could say would change the way I feel about you." He gazed over at her. She looked wide-eyed and puzzled.

"I just remember when Kaden kissed you, you were worried that I would somehow be mad at you. I want to make it clear..."

"Bryce, nothing happened. I promise," she interrupted.

"I'm letting you know, that if it did…"

"Nothing happened," Talia repeated more forcefully. She held his gaze. "Please, Bryce, you have to believe me."

"Thank God," he said, scooping her into his lap and nuzzling her neck. "I mean, I think I could tell Kaden was lying, but I couldn't be certain." He tightened his hold on her, but his mood didn't improve. The two sat in silence for what seemed like ages to Talia. Finally, she couldn't stand the tension any longer.

"There's something else, isn't there?" she asked. "Please, just tell me."

"Nothing. I can't. I just can't tell you."

"What? What can't you tell me?" She frowned. She wanted Bryce to trust her enough that he could tell her anything. "You just sat there and told me to be honest with you no matter what. I expect the same courtesy."

"If I tell you, I think you might hate me," he admitted.

"I could never hate you." She was surprised he could even think such a thing.

"I'm not so sure," he muttered.

Talia climbed off his lap and stood before him, leaning in close and locking her eyes with his. "Bryce, you can tell me anything. I promise you, there's nothing you could tell me that could possibly change the way I feel about you."

"I'm the reason you had to put up with Kaden," he blurted out. He had meant to introduce the fact with a little more finesse, but it was too late now. The words were out, and now Talia would hate him forever.

Talia took a step backwards. "What... what do you mean?"

"Kaden was my friend. He was running low on funds and needed work. I'm the one who gave him the job looking after the new Comforts. Looking after you." Bryce wanted to punch the wall in disgust.

Talia was speechless as she tried to process what Bryce had just revealed. So many emotions gushed through her.

"Please say something," he said after what seemed like an eternity. He braced himself for her to shout at him and tell him she hated him. He deserved it, and he knew he shouldn't have kept it a secret from her.

142

"Bryce," she, said hesitantly, but to his relief she didn't throw a punch or run from the room. She remained where she stood, her feet glued in place.

"Oh Talia, I know that I can never make it up to you. But if you'll forgive me, I'd like to try." Bryce had never begged anyone for anything, but he was willing to grovel if it meant convincing the woman he loved to stay.

She sat down beside him again. "There's nothing to forgive. You couldn't have known. I just feel bad that this is what you thought you couldn't tell me. The past is the past. You can't undo the years I spent with Kaden and I can't undo what he in turn did to Rachel. We both have guilt over this, but we can't let it spoil what we have now."

Bryce kissed her. He was both relieved and elated. He had been so convinced she'd leave him once she discovered the truth. He wanted to kiss away every hurt Kaden had ever bestowed on her – to undo every wrong done to her, right down to the small tattoo that his father's laws had forced on her shoulder blade. Then again, he loved that the tattoo was his family crest. To Bryce the swords represented the harsher side of his family heritage (his father, the previous kings, and even him, to some extent), while the angel wings embodied the softer side (his late grandmother, his mother, now Talia). Altogether it made a beautifully balanced picture of power and poise – the perfect parallel to his relationship with Talia. He absentmindedly traced the outline of the wings with his fingertips.

"I need you, Talia," he whispered. "Don't ever leave."

"Never," she promised, pressing her lips to his.

CHAPTER 23

THE PALACE GOSSIP soon died down, and before long speculation and false reports about what happened to Kaden and why he had tried to attack Bryce had dissipated. When rumors were at their worst, Talia and Bryce kept a low profile, dodging social events and even Bryce's own parents. But now the people of Inizi had something new to talk about – the growing mob of rebel protesters camped about the palace walls, demanding freedom and reform. While the prince was kept informed about the actions of the protesters, Talia remained blissfully unaware from the secure confines of Bryce's living quarters.

"Let's go to the ball tonight," Bryce suggested, showing the invitation to Talia.

"Really?" He could tell she was excited by the idea. "You think it'll be okay?"

"Yeah, and besides, what do we care what people think?"

"Speaking of that," she said, "what do you want me to call you around people?"

"What do you mean?"

"I mean you should have seen the look on Dr. Thomas' face when I called you by your first name. Not to mention your father's obvious disapproval."

"Talia," he said patiently, "I like it when you call me Bryce. I'm not seeking anyone's approval and you don't need to either. You can call me whatever makes you happy."

Her face lit up into a smile. "Can I call you *hot stuff*?"

"I find it suits me."

When Talia entered the ballroom with Bryce by her side, she felt all eyes on her. She glanced down at her midsection, self-conscious that she might be showing and worried that may be the reason for all the attention. Confident that her gown hid any small baby bump she might have, she shot Bryce a questioning look.

"Relax," he soothed. "They're just shocked that I've managed to bring the same woman to more than one event." He took her hand and led her onto the dance floor.

There was a time that Talia was certain she had two left feet, but dance lessons were one of many mandatory classes in the two-year education and refinement process of a Comfort. To her surprise, she'd discovered she enjoyed ballroom dancing; but never as much as this moment in Bryce's arms.

After several dances, Grace cut in to dance with her son, and Talia excused herself to grab a glass of water from the bar. She ran into

Chadwick, standing guard at the far corner of the room. "You on duty?" she asked him.

"Not really, but I like to keep an eye on things." His eyes brightened at seeing her. The dancing had left her slightly flushed and he wasn't sure if she'd ever looked more radiant.

"Well, since you're not really on duty," she told him, "I feel it's only right that you join me for a dance." He tried to protest, but she was already dragging him onto the dance floor.

The music number was upbeat, and Chad was relieved. He didn't think his heart could take a slow dance with her. He was finding it harder to keep his feelings at bay when he was near her; but he knew acting on his emotions would be a betrayal to both Bryce and to her. Talia swayed to the beat and he felt awkward in her presence, but still managed to have fun. She had an energy that made it hard not to.

"Thank you," she told him as he led her back to the corner of the room. The pair chatted for a few minutes before Talia was whisked onto the dance floor by another guest.

Talia thoroughly enjoyed herself that evening, although she saw little of Bryce, who was often pulled onto the dance floor by a pretty, young woman or could be seen politicking with some of the men. Talia didn't mind. She herself danced with several noblemen and conversed easily with Grace and some of the other guests. She marveled at how the alcohol and music made all the guests act more friendly and approachable.

She was at the bar, requesting another glass of water, when she spotted Bryce from across the room. She watched him as he walked towards her. His expression was intense – focused. As he drew closer, she wasn't sure what to expect. Had she done something wrong? Maybe he didn't like that she had danced with Chad earlier. Was he angry? When Bryce reached her side, he didn't say a word. He took the glass of water from her hand, placed it on the bar, then closed his hand over hers to guide her out of the room.

Talia allowed herself to be led down the dimly lit hallway, her heart hammering in her chest. Once they rounded the corner, Bryce pressed her against the wall and crushed his lips down hard on hers. "You look too good tonight for me to stay away from you any longer," he whispered fiercely in her ear.

Her pulse quickened, and her lips parted, inviting Bryce to sweep his tongue inside her mouth. Her body quivered with passion. Passion and relief: relief that Bryce whisked her away because he desired her, and not for anything that she had done wrong. She felt her eyes grow misty. Bryce must have noticed. "What's wrong, Talia," he asked, cupping her chin in his hand so that he could get a better look at her.

"Nothing," she whispered.

"No, tell me," he urged.

She felt awkward. "I thought you were angry with me. I guess I was sort of afraid..."

Bryce's jaw tightened. He hated that he could still frighten her. It was never his intention. "I couldn't be angry with you."

"Sometimes you are," she said, eyes wide. Bryce couldn't argue. Sometimes the woman drove him stark raving mad. But he would never hurt her.

"You are right," he said. "Sometimes you do make me angry. And I'm sure sometimes I make you angry."

Talia snorted in response. Bryce grinned and stroked her cheek with the back of his hand. "But no matter what," he continued, "you are safe with me. Always. Nothing you could ever do will change that."

She nodded in acceptance and leaned into him, pressing her cheek to his chest. He scooped her up in his arms and she squealed, giddy with happiness. When they reached the door to Bryce's quarters, Jamison was standing outside it. When he opened it for them, Talia felt herself flush. She knew it was obvious what she and Bryce would be doing once the door closed, but Jamison's face didn't reveal any judgement.

Bryce headed straight for the bed, setting Talia down before he kneeled down beside her. "We good?" he asked, still concerned about her fears moments before.

"Yes," she said, a little out of breath. Bryce looked doubtful. "Yes," she said again, this time with more conviction. "I love you Bryce," she told him, because she wanted to make sure he knew.

"I love you too," he told her. His movements were slower than they had been in the hallway. His urgency was still there, humming just beneath the surface, but he was gentler, his kisses tender. He slipped his hands under Talia's skirts and slid the folds of the fabric up and above her buttocks.

Talia laid her head back on the bed. Bryce stripped off his clothes before lying down next to her. He placed his hand on her cheek and leaned in to kiss her. He was naked, but she was still fully clothed, her skirts billowing around her waist and exposing her lacy panties. His graceful fingers loosened the buttons on the bodice of her gown, and her nipples hardened in response. If Bryce continued with his slow, calculated movements, Talia thought she might die.

"Please," she implored him.

He smiled. "Patience, love."

Talia lay naked next to Bryce, trying to catch her breath after their lovemaking, but without much success. Every part of her felt fulfilled and she cuddled up closer to him so she could feel his trembling body next to her own. "What made you think I would hurt you today?" he asked, breaking the tranquil silence.

"I don't think that," she told him. She was being honest. She now knew she could trust him. He had proven himself to her time and time again.

"Maybe not at this moment, but about an hour ago…"

She was silent. How could she explain to him how horrible Kaden had been? Especially now that she knew it was Bryce who had given him the job. It would kill him.

"It was Kaden, wasn't it?" he answered for her. Talia did her best to swallow the lump in her throat.

She turned to face him. "That has nothing to do with you."

"Don't," he said. "Don't try and make me feel better. I want to know what he did to you."

She said nothing. Instead she stared in earnest into the deep blue of Bryce's eyes, pondering how to respond.

"Talia, every time you flinch at my movements, every time you cringe at my touch, it kills me. I know somehow, I did that. That's on me. So please – please help me understand what happened to you." When Bryce reached up to tuck a strand of hair behind Talia's ear, she noticed the tremor of his hand.

"I just want to put it behind me," she said.

"I know you do, *ameerah*," he soothed. "But the sooner you open up about it, the sooner we can move past it." His logic made sense, but she knew that unloading her afflictions would increase the burden of guilt Bryce already carried. She couldn't do that to him.

"You're still worried about me," he said, as if reading her thoughts. She sighed but didn't answer. "Listen, don't worry about me. I have come to terms that there are some things I cannot change. However, I can help make amends by helping you get over what you experienced."

Bryce sat up in bed, pulling Talia into a seated position. He faced her, clasping both of her hands in his. "Lay it on me," he said, more light-heartedly, and Talia couldn't help but laugh. She took a deep, deliberate breath and started to speak.

"Since the first time I came to the palace, Kaden set his sights on me..." Bryce listened intently as she began to describe the two years she spent with Kaden and his cruel acts of punishment she'd endured. More than once Talia saw the flash of anger in Bryce's eyes, and felt him squeeze her hands in his, but she continued.

"There was one time that I allowed myself to trust him," she continued. "I had clumsily knocked over some hideous statue in the outer courtyard and it broke. Kaden sent me up to my room, threatening to punish me for not behaving like a lady. He always had some sort of excuse for his sadistic punishments. He didn't come to my room that night, and I don't know if I made myself sick with worry, or if it was a coincidence, but when Kaden finally did come up to my room the next morning, I was sicker than I had ever been."

Bryce listened with a growing, queasy feeling in the pit of his stomach as her story unfolded.

࿓࿓࿓

"Are you ready to accept your punishment?" Kaden asked cruelly from Talia's bedroom doorway. He started to unfasten his belt buckle, but Talia remained in bed, the covers pulled up to her chin.

"Kaden, please, I'm not asking you not to punish me, but can you please do it later? I am so sick." She sounded tired, groggy. She groaned and curled up in a ball, clutching her stomach. At first Kaden thought she was acting, but as he got closer he could see the sweat across her forehead. Her skin was pale and pasty.

"What's wrong?" he said, stopping in his tracks.

"I'm not sure. I might have the flu." She sounded miserable.

Kaden felt her forehead. She was burning up. He summoned one of the other Comforts to bring up broth and some medicine. When it arrived, Kaden climbed into bed with her, fully clothed, and helped her sit up to sip the broth.

"You need to get something in your system," he coaxed. But after Talia had eaten the broth, she sat straight up and vomited over the side of the bed. She thought Kaden would be angry, but instead he held back her hair as she emptied the contents of her stomach. He then disappeared and returned with a bowl and a towel.

He dropped the towel over the vomit on the floor, a temporary solution until the servants could clean it up, placed the bowl on the small nightstand, and once again climbed back into bed with her. There was nothing sexual about it – his actions were gentle and kind. Each time Talia sat up to vomit, Kaden supported the bowl in one hand and held back her hair with the other.

"Will you stay with me?" she asked, leaning into him for support.

Over the next few days, Kaden barely left Talia's side except to eat, sleep, or to step out of the room while one of the servants gave her a sponge bath and washed her hair. As she lay there with him, letting him dab her forehead with a wet rag, she wondered if she'd pegged him all wrong. Perhaps he could be gentle and good. She allowed him to cradle her in his arms as she rested her head on his chest. It was the first time since before her parents' death that she'd felt comfort from being close to someone.

By day four, Talia finally started to feel better. She arose from bed and tidied up the room. Kaden had ordered servants to clean her room and provide fresh bedsheets daily, so there wasn't much to do, but she couldn't stand staying in bed any longer. She crossed the room to the small mirror and proceeded to coax her hair into a tight braid. It was then that Kaden knocked softly and entered the room.

"How are you feeling?" he asked. Talia smiled at him, grateful for the kindness he'd shown her.

"Much better, thank you." She took a step towards him but stopped when she noticed his changed expression.

"That's good," he said, "now I can finally punish you." As he'd done days earlier, he reached down to unsheathe his belt and Talia felt herself shrink against the wall. She watched helplessly as the leather strap sprung from the captivity of his belt loops.

"Kaden, please…" but her pleas were in vain.

"Now Talia, you know it's only fair. After all, I only promised to wait until you felt better. And I've been a patient man waiting for that to happen." Kaden held his belt in one hand like a whip, the end trailing on the floor. As he drew closer, he folded the belt in half, slapping the folded end against his open palm and sneering. He was taunting her, and Talia realized with revulsion that he actually enjoyed this – he got off on it.

Horrified, she tried to flee, but she stumbled against the corner of the dresser, knocking over a porcelain jewelry box and sending it crashing to the floor. It was the only thing Talia owned that had belonged to her mother, one of the few surviving articles from the fire, but she didn't have time to mourn the loss of her most prized possession. Kaden made a clucking sound with his tongue.

"Isn't your clumsiness what brought me here in the first place?" Talia wanted to tell him that the real reason he was there was because he was a sick bastard, but she held her tongue, and her breath, as she waited for the first blow.

Typically, she took her punishment in silence, but this time the pain was unbearable. She couldn't be sure if she was still weak from her illness, or if Kaden put days of pent-up frustration behind each swing, but she found herself begging for mercy each time the leather struck her skin. She kept her eyes squeezed shut as her mind tried to comprehend that the man, who in the days earlier had shown her such kindness, was the same man now inflicting so much pain. And each time she cried out, Kaden smiled with smug satisfaction. When he left the room, Talia remained huddled on the floor, tormented by her own confusion, pain, and humiliation.

"When I finally managed to pick myself up off the floor, I had to spend the next two days in bed," Talia finished. "And I learned to never trust again – to never rely on anyone for anything. Until you, that is."

Her cheeks were wet with tears, but she felt a profound sense of relief at confiding her past to Bryce. He was silent as he tried to reconcile his childhood friend with the monster Talia just described. She scooted closer to him, unsettled by the silence. "Please say something," she said.

The prince swallowed hard, doing his best to process everything Talia had just told him. What she'd had to endure was far worse than he had imagined. He wondered why she didn't hate him. He didn't deserve her. "I am... so sorry," he started, but Talia covered his mouth with hers.

Gently pulling away, Bryce reached out for her hand, setting it against his own hand that he in turn placed on her damp cheek. With Talia's hand guiding his, Bryce stroked her cheek. He leaned in and kissed her shoulder.

"Lay down on your stomach," he whispered in her ear. Her heart was racing, but she obeyed. He knelt on the bed beside her trembling body and began to knead her soft skin with his fingertips. She sighed, her body relaxing, as his nimble fingers massaged her shoulders and worked their way to the small of her back. The caress from his fingertips tickled her skin and stirred her senses.

"I only want to touch you to bring you comfort and pleasure – never pain," he told her. His tone was intense, wounded, and Talia rolled over onto her back to face him again.

"I know now that you would never hurt me," she said, lifting her head to kiss him again. "I trust you. I love you. Please, please let's put this behind us; for both of our sakes."

Bryce knew that a part of him would always hate himself for what Talia had endured, but he would keep those feelings locked away if it meant she wouldn't have to think about those experiences ever again. "Okay. Okay we will," he told her. "God, I don't deserve you though." He pulled her close, silently praying for her forgiveness.

"I disagree," she told him. "You saved me, in so many ways."

Bryce said nothing. What he wanted to tell her, without admitting how lost he was before, was that in actuality she saved him. She. Saved. Him.

CHAPTER 24

RETURNING EARLY from his trip to surprise her, Bryce stared at Talia through the window of the coffee shop. She leaned in closer to read her book and a small strand of dark hair fell over her left eye. Something she read made her smile and watching her look so carefree made Bryce smile too. She lifted the coffee mug to her lips and sipped the hot substance, closing her eyes in obvious enjoyment. Bryce hesitated at the door of the coffee shop, one hand on the door handle. He longed to be near her but didn't want to disturb the tranquil scene.

Spotting him through the glass door, Talia smiled, set down the mug, and motioned him over. "What are you reading?" he asked, taking a seat across from her.

"Oh, it's nothing," she said, closing the book and placing it on the table, cover-side down. She flashed a sheepish grin and her cheeks flushed.

"Someone looks guilty," Bryce mused, turning over the book so he could read the cover. "Is this a romance novel?"

She flushed again. "Your mother lent it to me. She picked it up at the antique store."

"Disturbing," he teased. "You know they have these electronic now. Have for quite some time."

"I still prefer the paperback novel. There's something about the smell of the weathered paper, being able to earmark the pages, and seeing the words in clear print." Her eyes were gleaming.

"Is there any advice I could glean from the leading man in this book?"

"Nah, he's got nothing on you." She plucked the book from his grasp and planted a swift kiss on his cheek.

Switching the subject, she asked, "How was your trip?"

"Oh, it was good. Business is proceeding as planned." Bryce never revealed much about his trips. Talia took it to mean he didn't much like what he did and didn't want to bore her with the details. In actuality, he had a deep passion for what he was trying to accomplish. He wouldn't let business keep him away from Talia for anything he didn't deem important. Truth be told, he left out details to protect her, but he hated to be so vague. His omissions made him feel disloyal somehow, and the guilt weighed on him. But he reminded himself that the end would justify the means. Maybe. Hopefully.

"You're back, but still so far away," Talia said. She made a funny face to grab his attention.

He smiled. "Sorry. I'm back. What would you like to do now that you have me to yourself?" He leaned in closer, undressing her with his eyes as if they were the only two people in the coffee shop. Talia squirmed in her seat.

"Back to our room?" he suggested, and she smiled in agreement. She happily wondered when it became *their* room.

"You've been doing some redecorating," he observed when they entered their shared living quarters. He sounded amused, but not at all like he minded.

"Well, your mother and I both felt that it needed a woman's touch."

"My mom meddles," Bryce said. But he smiled to himself. The bond Talia and his mother formed pleased him to no end.

Talia wrestled with the zipper of her gown and Bryce offered to help her. "I'd hate to say it," she said, "but I may need to invest in some maternity clothes. Or at least the next size up."

He smiled, helping her the rest of the way out of her gown. He stepped back to study her. Every part of her was slender, including her stomach, although if he looked closely he could see it protruding ever so slightly. "What are we, about three months now?"

"About that," she said, elated that he was keeping track and used the term *we*.

"I'm just thankful the morning sickness is subsiding," she confessed, making a face.

Bryce agreed whole-heartedly. It had been hard for him to see her so miserable, morning after morning. It made him feel helpless.

"We should find out what we're having in a couple of weeks," she said. "Dr. Thomas said to let him know a date and time that worked for us and he can come up."

"We haven't talked about what we want," Bryce observed. "Boy or a girl?"

"Healthy," Talia corrected.

"That's what everyone says," he laughed. "But most people still have a preference."

Talia would like nothing more than to give Bryce a boy to carry on his family name. But she knew the kingdom would never let the *bastard* son of a Comfort succeed the throne, so she hoped with everything within her that they were having a girl. She didn't want Bryce, or her baby, to endure that sort of conflict or rejection.

Bryce studied her, wondering why she looked so sad when it should be a happy occasion.

"What would you prefer?" she asked, still not answering him.

"Really, I'm good with either. I know whatever we have, boy or girl, our baby will be perfect."

He wrapped her in his arms and planted a chaste kiss on her lips. "Make the appointment for two weeks from today," he told her. "I'm only back for a couple of days and have to go on a short trip again."

Talia's face fell, and she pulled back from him. "I know, I know," he told her, "but I promise things will slow down soon. I won't be gone that long. Soon you'll have me around more than you can stand."

Talia was doubtful, but she smiled and pretended to believe him.

"You know, pretty soon we'll have to tell people about the baby," she said shyly, nervous what his reaction might be. Despite her hints, they'd never discussed how they would announce the pregnancy. "People are going to take notice once I start waddling through the halls."

"We will. I have a plan," he told her, his cheerful expression unchanging. He patted her stomach and talked at her midsection. "You'll just have to stay a secret for a short while longer."

"You're not worried about how your parents will react?"

"Not really." He shrugged.

"That's about all I think about."

Bryce took her in his arms once more. He hadn't realized how much the subject had been weighing on her. "I think my mom will be thrilled." He kissed the top of her head, then cupped her chin in his hand. "And my dad? Well, he'll have to get over it."

His casual demeanor was a load off Talia's mind. "Thank you for loving me," she told him. Then she patted her stomach. "Thank you for loving us." Bryce melted at her sincerity. She really had no idea how easy she was to love.

CHAPTER 25

TALIA AWOKE to voices arguing in the hallway. Curious, she crept out of bed and pressed her ear to the wall by the doorway.

"You have to be willing to make a change, *Dad*," she heard Bryce say.

"I don't have to do anything, *Son*," the king hissed.

"Why won't you listen to reason? Your people aren't going to be content with living in squalor, with no hope of pulling themselves out. You have to offer them solutions."

"Why don't you let me worry about *my* people?"

"A good leader is wise enough to know he's not the only one with good ideas," Bryce shouted. Talia could hear the rattling of the bedroom door handle, so she scrambled away from the wall and back into bed.

Bryce barged into the room and slammed the door behind him. He sighed in disgust.

"What was that about?" she asked, unable to help herself.

"It just means I have more work ahead of me than I realized," he muttered. Talia's heart landed in her stomach. *More work? What did that mean? He was away on business so much already.*

When Bryce left town again, Talia didn't waste any time springing into action. She'd been thinking long and hard about how to ensure her baby had the brightest future and was accepted amongst society. She also could no longer bear the guilt that the Comforts were left in such unfortunate circumstances while she rubbed elbows with the nobles and got to return to the same bed every night. She was determined to come up with a solution to help her baby and her friends.

She opened the bedchamber door and found Chad in the hallway, faithful as always. "I need you to take me back to Building A," she told him.

"Talia, we've been through this. You belong here."

"I need to see my friends," she explained. He looked hesitant. "Please, Chad, I want to see how they're doing and I have some questions for them. It's for a little research project I'm doing." He still wasn't thrilled with the idea but agreed to take her.

Arriving at Building A, Talia knocked on the door. Sasha answered, looking both Talia and Chadwick up and down. "Selection time isn't until 7 p.m.," she said pointedly to Chadwick. "And we don't accept returns." Despite her cool demeanor, Talia noticed a peculiar, unexpected half-smile.

Chadwick laughed and embraced Sasha in a bear hug. *Strange.* Talia hadn't realized they'd become friends.

At hearing the news of Talia's arrival, the Comforts gathered in the great room. There was a flurry of excitement. Naturally, most women wanted to know more about Talia (something to confirm the circulating rumors), but they also wanted to know the purpose of her visit.

Once Talia revealed her intention to conduct interviews, she was met with skepticism and several probing questions. Her responses were vague, not wishing to get anyone's hopes up. But she did squash rumors that she was there in a spying capacity for the royal family and assured everyone she had their best interests at heart.

"If you'll just trust me, all will soon be revealed."

Still skeptical, some of the Comforts refused to be interviewed, but most agreed. While the women patiently waited in the great room, Talia set up shop in the drawing room so her interviews could be conducted in private. With it being located just beyond the great room, the ladies could have a spacious, comfortable place to assemble while they waited.

Armed with a tablet complete with voice transcription, Talia invited anyone willing to participate to be interviewed one-on-one. She took a seat in one of the wingback chairs, leaving the couch for the interview participants. She set out candies and tea to make the interviewees feel more at ease.

Sephora was one of the first to be interviewed. Talia was a bundle of nerves, uncertain how her questions would be received, but when Sephora stepped into the room, she brought with her a great calm. Beyond her exotic beauty, Sephora had a natural air of grace that reached beyond what could be taught.

"It's nice to see you," Sephora said. She seemed to float in her flowy, jade-colored gown as she made her way across the room. She offered Talia a peck on the cheek, then sat upright across from her, crossing her legs at the ankles.

"It's great seeing you," Talia said. "How are you getting along?" The question wasn't part of the interview. Talia felt genuine concern for the beautiful creature she'd always held in high regard.

Sephora dipped her head slightly but smiled. "I am doing as well as can be expected," she said. Her tone held no emotion. No bitterness.

"Well, if you're ready, I think we'll start the interview now."

"I'm ready."

Talia pressed her lips together, drawing on her courage. Sephora had always been a private person, so she hoped her questions wouldn't be too intrusive.

"If you were free to do as you choose, what hobbies interest you?"

"I like to tell myself I am free to choose," Sephora said, laughing nervously and appearing a bit rattled for the first time.

Talia remained silent. As she suspected, sharing personal information didn't come easily for Sephora.

Realizing she wasn't going to get out of answering the question, Sephora began. "When I was a little girl, my daddy taught me to dance. In our house there wasn't much money, but there was laughter, music – and there was always dancing." She paused in poignant remembrance. "I'd go out dancing," she decided.

"I'll bet you're a wonderful dancer," Talia told her. She'd never known Sephora to be anything but graceful.

Sephora smiled. "My mum always said I was a natural."

Talia wanted to ask about Sephora's family, but she knew her friend wasn't ready to get that personal. "What else?" she finally asked. "What other hidden talents do you possess that you haven't shared?" Talia's tone and mood were lighter. Her interview now felt more like a casual conversation.

Sephora smiled again and thought for a moment. "I also knit."

"Knit?" Talia couldn't hide the surprise she felt. Knitting hadn't been practiced in decades – at least not that she'd heard of.

"I know, strange, right? I used to suffer from a lot of anxiety. I found knitting keeps me calm."

Talia stared over at her, trying to picture Sephora as anything other than serene. "That's amazing," she finally said. "Okay, now let's talk jobs."

"Jobs?"

"This question requires you to dig down deep," Talia laughed, and Sephora made an adorable scrunchy face in response. "If you could be anything you wanted to be, what would it be?"

"Are we talking occupations?"

Talia nodded.

Sephora paused to consider, but Talia suspected it wasn't the first time she had pondered this question. "I've always loved children," she revealed. "My dream is to run a center to help underprivileged children. A place where kids could come to feel safe. And loved." Sephora's cheeks glowed pink through her caramel-toned skin and a small tear hovered in the corner of her eye.

"That's amazing," Talia told her. "Really, really beautiful."

"What about you?" Sephora asked, catching Talia off guard.

"Pardon?" she asked, stalling for time.

"What would you be?"

Talia smiled. "Something in politics. Or charitable work. Nothing specific – I just want to make a difference. I want to do something that would have made my parents proud."

"I'd say you're doing that right now," Sephora said.

Once she swapped back to interviewee mode, Sephora soared through the final questions, opening up about her dreams and aspirations. Both ladies found it hard for the interview to be over. They stood to their feet and embraced each other before Sephora made a smooth exit and called in the next person.

Although each interview had a unique flavor, Talia was careful to ask the same list of questions of each participant; adequately covering skillset, talents, hobbies, and what constituted a dream job in their mind. Chad was a good sport, hanging around without complaint – though Talia suspected he might be sticking around to spend time with Sasha. She decided the two would make an adorable pair. Perhaps Sasha was the mystery lady Bryce mentioned.

Talia was about an hour into her interviews when she looked up and saw Rachel filing in. "Thank you for meeting with me today," Talia told her.

Rachel smiled, but it seemed forced. "I guess I should thank you for getting rid of Kaden," she said. Her tone was laced with bitterness.

"I didn't have much to do with that."

"Then I guess we're done here," she said, rising from her chair.

"No, Rachel, wait. I'm sorry. Please take a seat. If I want you to be honest with me, I need to be honest with you. You're right, I was involved; but Bryce, err, the prince, ensured Kaden paid for his past crimes."

This time when Rachel smiled, it was genuine. "Well, I truly am thankful. Now fire away."

Talia took a deep breath and cleared her throat before beginning the interview. Even more so than the rest, she wanted to be sure she got this interview right. She started off with an easy question. "In what township were you born?"

"Starlings," Rachel answered. "On the east side," she said with an air of snobbery. The east side of Starlings was as close to middleclass as any of the townships Talia had ever heard of.

"Impressive," Talia said, smiling – but in the back of her mind flashed the question: *then why did your parents take the money over you?*

"If you could live anywhere in Inizi, where would that be?" she continued.

"Now that Kaden isn't around, I'd say living within the palace walls suits me just fine."

Talia felt some relief, but also wondered if Rachel lacked imagination. "And what about a job?"

"What do you mean?" Her tone held a hint of suspicion.

"I mean, if your circumstances were different, and you could have any job you wanted, what would it be?"

"I'd be a firefighter," Rachel said. Talia almost burst out laughing, assuming she was teasing, but Rachel's confident expression confirmed her answer wasn't in jest. Perhaps Rachel had more spirit and imagination than Talia gave her credit for.

After completing the interviews in Building A, where Talia learned more about the Comforts in a span of a few hours than she had over the past two years, she and Chad moved on to buildings B and C. Although most occupants were willing to participate, Talia found the women far less enthusiastic about her questions. To her surprise, most claimed to enjoy their lifestyle and said they had no aspirations of a career. Many thumbed their noses at the idea of holding down a job and paying rent.

"I don't know if I should feel sorry for those women, or feel relief," she told Chad once they'd finished the interviews in the latter two buildings.

Chad frowned. "If Bryce heard their responses, it might absolve him of some of the guilt he carries, but I can't rightly say if those women genuinely feel that way or have been so beaten down they can't fathom having a life of their own. I guess it would be like being in prison for most of your adult life. Studies show that once inmates with twenty or more years under their belt are released, they often re-offend in a short period because they don't know what to do with themselves in the real world."

Talia pondered this information in silence.

"Where to next?" he asked, changing the subject.

"Well, I'm starving, so I thought we might grab a bite to eat. Then I'd like to go back to my room to consolidate my data."

On the short walk to the restaurant Talia heard a loud commotion outside the palace walls. "What is that?" she asked. "It sounds like a crowd, chanting."

Chadwick looked uncomfortable. "There's been a bit of unrest amongst the townspeople."

"What do you mean by unrest?"

"It's nothing to be concerned with," he said, kicking the cobblestone as they walked and avoiding her gaze.

"Chad," she said, coming to a stop. "I have a right to know what's going on."

"I'll show you," he said, giving in. He took her by the hand and led her to a watch tower, where she stared in worry at the tall ladder that scaled to the top.

"Don't worry," he told her, grinning at her horrified reaction to the narrow ladder. "There's a lift."

Chad nodded to the guard stationed next to the lift and the guard nodded back before stepping aside. Escorting Talia inside, Chad pushed the button for the observation deck. Despite her mild fear of heights, Talia stepped forward to watch the view from the glass front of the lift as it ascended the twenty stories to the top.

When they reached their destination and the lift doors opened, the pair made their way onto the observation deck. Chad led Talia to a nearby looking post. Using a telescope mounted between the battlements, she surveyed the crowd below. Hundreds lined the outer palace walls, wearing white armbands with some sort of flower she couldn't make out, holding up signs, and chanting in unison. Talia focused on the signs. Each held a message demanding reform.

"What is this about?" she asked.

"Is this the first you've seen this?" Chad hadn't realized until this moment how sheltered she had been.

When Talia shook her head, he continued. "The people that live outside these walls are restless. They are tired of being ruled over and not having a voice." Talia glanced up at him, surprised by his candor. "That's at least what I've heard," he finished.

"Will they be arrested?" she asked, noticing the palace guards and Inizi peace officers that flanked the crowd. She also knew there were several laws against open criticism of the royal family.

"No. They have a permit for peaceful assembly, so as long as they protest an actual cause, without directly disparaging the king – and of course, as long as they're not violent."

"*Are* they violent?"

"No," Chad answered in a tone more forceful than he intended. "At least, most of them aren't," he said, softening his tone. "Most of them just want to be heard. The white armbands they wear actually symbolize peace. The flower is the Royal Bluebell and many speculate it represents what the monarchy could be if the people were given more of a voice."

Talia was somber on the ride down the lift. She knew most of that anger was directed at the king, but she wondered how much of it was misplaced towards Bryce and his mother.

"Bryce is handling this," Chad assured her in response to her silence.

"So, he knows?" Part of her hoped that, with Bryce's heavy travel schedule, he was unaware of the protestors.

170

"Of course he knows," he chuckled. "He's on top of it, and, in a way, you could say he supports it."

"What does that mean?"

Chad paused, fearing he'd already said too much. "All I can say is, he's got it handled and wouldn't want you to worry about it. Or mention it," he said, shooting her a warning look.

She nodded. "Then let's do lunch," she said. She was willing to drop the subject. For now.

"So, what's up with you and Sasha?" she asked at lunch. Her question took Chad by surprise, making him blush.

"Who says there's anything going on with me and Sasha?"

"I say."

"Well, she makes me laugh," Chad offered. "She has a fascinating sense of humor. We're mostly just friends. But I don't know, maybe…"

"Sense of humor, huh?" Talia looked doubtful.

Chad grinned at her. "She's a bit rough around the edges, but once you get past that, her softer, witty side comes out. She's had some tough breaks."

"Really, like what?" Talia hoped she wasn't being too forward.

"Well, she was married once. She's now widowed. Her husband didn't leave her with much, which is how she ended up a house matron."

"How sad, I didn't realize that. Now I feel bad that I didn't try to get to know her better."

"Nah, don't feel bad. I know she likes you. She told me."

Talia grinned. "Well, good. Now you can tell her the feeling is mutual."

After lunch, Chad escorted Talia back to her room.

"Where do you want to start tomorrow?" he asked, sensing her mission involving her friends was far from over.

She smiled at him. "How about an early start? Breakfast, then we can head to the palace library? I'd like to do some more research and I'd bet money they have a data simulator I can put all my information into."

Chad nodded. "Okay, I'll come get you in the morning. Say, seven-thirty?"

Talia nodded, then cast a longing glance at the tablet that held her interview notes, so Chad said his goodnights and showed himself out.

"I've been checking in on the other Comforts while you've been gone," Talia said over breakfast once Bryce returned from his trip. He seemed more tired than usual and she did her best to carry the conversation. "Rachel is doing well."

Her revelation was followed by a long, silent pause. "I don't want you going there anymore," Bryce finally said.

Talia looked up from her breakfast plate in surprise, swallowing a bite of toast before responding. "Why?"

"Because I don't want you to be reminded of that part of your life. It's not who you are anymore."

She sprang from her chair. "That will *always* be a part of who I am."

"You know what I mean," he said, growing tense. He pushed the eggs around on his plate with his fork while he worked to summon his patience.

"No, I'm not sure that I do know." She crossed her arms in defiance, testing him.

"Dammit I am sick of everything being a fight." Bryce pounded his fist on the table as he rose from his chair – rattling the juice goblets and startling Talia. Realizing he'd frightened her, he stepped towards her to apologize, but she winced and took a step back. He could almost physically see her working out her escape path in her head, and it frustrated him. He'd tried to be patient; especially given that he'd unintentionally orchestrated the events that led to her distrust. But how many times could he show her she was safe with him?

When he took another step towards her, she yelped and turned to run, knocking over the mosaic glass vase in her path. It shattered into a million, tiny pieces on the tile floor. Hearing the commotion, Chad rushed in, unannounced and uninvited. He glanced from Bryce to Talia.

The prince stood over Talia, who was kneeling on the floor, collecting the larger pieces of the vase in her trembling hands. "I'm sorry, it's not that I don't trust you," Chad heard her explain to Bryce. "It's just a reaction. A reflex."

"Personally, I don't think she needs to apologize for anything," Chad interrupted. His anger towards Bryce was evident.

"You forget yourself Chadwick," Bryce warned and Talia's cheeks glowed pink.

Ignoring, him, Chad crouched next to Talia and helped her sift through the glass. It was a pointless task, but he deduced she needed the time to sort out her feelings more than anything.

"Leave it," Bryce said, annoyed at how the situation had spiraled out of his control.

Talia and Chad stood to their feet, disposing the glass shards they'd collected into the trash bin.

"You can see that she's okay, so you can leave now," Bryce said, glaring in Chad's direction and pointing towards the door.

Chad cleared his throat, wanting to say more, but instead he took Talia's hand in his. "I'll be right outside," he assured her before making his exit.

"I want to be perfectly clear," Bryce said, maintaining an even tone despite the anger bubbling in his gut. "I am not going to hurt you. I would never hit a woman – especially not you. I think you should know that by now. Sometimes we're going to argue, and that's okay. But I do feel responsible for your well-being, and for that of my unborn child, so I am telling you..." he paused and closed his eyes, then opened them again. "I am *asking* you," he corrected, "not to go visit the Comforts. At least for now. Can you do that for me?"

Talia nodded solemnly, swallowing the large lump forming in her throat.

"Thank you," he said. "Now I have a lot of work to do today, so I will see you later this evening." He walked over to her, kissed her cheek, then left the room. His kiss was cold, without feeling, and Talia sunk to the floor, falling to pieces next to the shattered urn.

"You're with me today," Bryce barked at Chad as he stepped into the hallway. "Ask Jamison to watch over Talia."

"Bryce," Chad started to say, but the prince shot him a warning glance. "Sir," he started again. "I'm sorry. You know I was just protecting her."

"I wasn't going to hurt her," Bryce said. The pain in his eyes was evident.

"I know that, sir. And I think Talia knows that. She's been through so much, and I don't want to let her down."

"You like her." It wasn't a question, and his statement held an inflection of bitterness.

"Of course I like her. Everyone likes her."

"You know what I mean."

Chad offered a blank stare, but his cheeks reddened. "I would never do anything to jeopardize your relationship with Talia," he finally said.

"That wasn't a denial."

"Would you like me to step down, sir?" Now it was Chad's turn to be angry.

"No," Bryce sighed. "Sorry Chad. Stop calling me *sir*. Once again I'm acting like a jealous lunatic."

"I'll notify Jamison that he's on point today for Talia," Chad said, not responding to Bryce's apology. Then he headed down the hall to relay the message.

Bryce returned to the room far later than usual. When he finally did arrive, his demeanor remained cool and Talia was beside herself. She'd waited around the room all day, not wanting to miss when he returned.

"Can we pretend this morning didn't happen?" she pleaded. When he didn't respond, she tried to lighten the mood. "At a minimum, I think we can both agree that I don't have a stellar track record with vases."

Bryce sighed, but offered her a faint smile. "I'm not trying to forbid you from anything," he explained. "There's some things going on that I need to protect you from."

"Okay, I understand," she said. She wondered if his concern had anything to do with the protestors she'd witnessed a few days earlier.

He sat on the edge of the bed and patted the mattress as an invitation for her to join him. She sat down next to him, resting her head on his shoulder. He leaned down and rested his head on hers. He felt drained. A thousand worries ran through his mind. "I love you, Talia," he finally said.

"I know, me too," she murmured.

And they sat that way in contented silence until forgiveness for the day's earlier events washed over them, cleansing their anger and regret.

CHAPTER 26

"OPEN CELL BLOCK TWO," Bryce barked, startling the prison guard on duty. Daylight had scarcely broken through and the guard wasn't used to receiving such early visitors – and never royalty.

"Yes sir," the man said, scrambling to his feet. He'd been notified there would be a prison transport, but nothing prepared him for a visit from the prince at such an ungodly hour.

"Thank you," Bryce said, softening his tone. He realized he had a tendency to be demanding, but he supposed that came with the territory.

When the two men arrived outside cell block two, the guard punched a code into the keypad on the wall, then placed his thumbprint on the device. The door swung open and he stepped aside to allow Bryce entrance.

Kaden sat on his bed in the corner of his cell, reading a book. His right ankle was cuffed to a long chain attached to the wall. He looked up at Bryce with indifference. "What are you doing here?" he asked. His tone suggested only mild interest.

"I'm here to hold up my end of the bargain. I have a plane waiting to take you to Australia."

Kaden's face fell, but he quickly recovered. "I thought I would remain here. On the island."

"I wouldn't let you within a hundred miles of Talia," Bryce said. "I would have sent you away further, but your parents begged me to reconsider. I have contacts in Australia who are willing to give you work. And keep an eye on you."

"I see your little girlfriend is still calling all the shots," Kaden taunted.

Bryce glowered down at the man he used to call his friend. "Kaden, our years of *friendship* (he tried not to choke on the word) is the only reason things aren't much worse for you. I misjudged you, and the woman I love paid a high price for it. I won't make that mistake again."

"The woman you love?" he scoffed. "And tell me, does she love you back? Or is she plotting revenge since you're the one that caused our paths to cross."

The prince remained calm, confident in Talia's affection for him, and that she had forgiven him. "Talia knows everything. There aren't any secrets between us. Or blame," he said pointedly.

"If you say so."

"Please handcuff him and escort him to the plane on the transport deck," Bryce told the prison guard. "I want him off this island and out of my sight."

Without a backwards glance, Bryce walked away, forever severing the tie with his childhood confidant.

In a celebratory mood, Bryce made reservations at *Kizzy-Anne's*, one of his favorite palace restaurants. The restaurant offered a bit of everything – seafood, steaks, Italian. Even the most influential families waited months to get a table, but Bryce simply made one phone call. He speculated his last-minute request may have bumped a family or two, but tonight he was feeling impulsive and selfish and didn't care.

Talia looked beautiful in a red, silk gown. It was lower-cut and fit her backside more snugly than the palace dress code typically allowed. Bryce loved it. She looked innocent and mouth-watering all at once.

"He's out of our lives for good now," he told her once they were alone and seated in a cozy corner of the restaurant.

"Really?" She looked relieved. She didn't have to ask whom he was referring to.

He reached across the table and took her hand in his. "We can put all this behind us, sweetie."

She beamed back at him. "I already have."

The waiter bustled over to take their drink orders. "A bottle of champagne to celebrate," Bryce said, but then caught himself, realizing Talia wouldn't be able to partake. "Actually, how about two glasses of sparkling cider instead."

"Very good, sir," the waiter said before he scurried away.

"What are you smiling about?" he asked when they were alone again.

Talia laughed. "I think it's funny how nervous you make everyone. I know you don't mean to, that's what makes it sort of comical."

"Do I make you nervous?" he teased, leaning in to kiss her from across the table.

"No," she decided. "Anxious. Stimulated. But not nervous."

"Stimulated. Hmm. Check please," he said aloud, to no one, and Talia laughed again.

"Perhaps we can order our food to go," she suggested.

CHAPTER 27

"DO YOU REALLY have to leave town again?" Talia pouted. She was sitting up in bed while Bryce rummaged around the bedroom for his other shoe. The couple had been quick to undress the night before and articles of clothing lay scattered across the bedroom floor.

"Sweetie, we've been over this," he said, taking a seat next to her on the bed. His tone wasn't impatient, only regretful.

"I know, I just miss you," she told him. "I'm thinking of getting a job to occupy my time."

"I'm sorry, are we running low on funds?"

Talia tossed a pillow at him. "I get bored waiting around sometimes. And you asked me not to visit the Comforts, so now..."

Bryce held his breath, hoping an argument wasn't brewing.

"What sort of job?" he asked.

"I was thinking of the antique store," she said. "I love it there, and I think they can use the help getting more organized."

"Let's talk about it when I get back."

Talia's face fell, presuming he was dismissing her idea. "Okay," she said, closing into herself.

"I think you should absolutely do it," Bryce clarified. "I just need to make sure we have your security detail worked out," he explained.

Face lighting up, she wrapped her arms around his neck and kissed him chastely. "Thank you, thank you." She was unable to contain her excitement.

"I've never seen anyone so happy to go to work," he laughed. "You won't be lifting heavy objects or staying on your feet too long, right?"

"I'll be careful," Talia promised. She rubbed her tiny baby bump and smiled to herself.

Bryce kissed her, then kissed her stomach before he finished getting dressed and headed out the door.

"Chad, I have a huge favor to ask," Talia said, opening the bedroom door and inviting him in.

"Anything. Name it." Chad hovered in the doorway, not wanting any appearances of impropriety. He'd already fended off some rumors he hoped never reached Talia. Or Bryce.

"I wonder if you could get me a meeting with the king," she said. She bit her lip and raised an eyebrow, aware of the magnitude of what she was asking.

"Name anything but that," he laughed.

"I'm being serious. Can you do it?"

"When?" He sounded a bit doubtful.

"As soon as possible. Preferably while Bryce is still out of town." She could tell her request made him uncomfortable.

"It's not that I'm trying to go behind his back," she explained. "It's just that this is something I want to do on my own. Bryce thinks he has to protect me from everything and I want to show him that..."

"I'll do it," Chad said. He knew and understood Talia's craving for independence and the need to prove herself. She was like a beautiful, exotic bird that shouldn't be caged. "Wait here and I'll find out when a meeting can be arranged."

Talia nervously paced the bedroom floor. She heard two sharp knocks on the door, followed by Chad's much anticipated arrival. "Well, what did he say?" she asked.

"He said he's willing to meet with you."

"When?"

"Now."

"Now?" Suddenly she was more nervous than ever before.

"You've got this," Chad said. "Bryce would be proud of the preparation you put into this," he added, though he was certain the prince would strangle him if he discovered he had gone behind his back and arranged a meeting with the king. Bryce probably trusted his father less than anyone.

Beaming at the compliment, but still aflutter with nerves, Talia gathered up her audiovisual equipment and traipsed behind Chad as he led the way to the king's chamber. One of the king's guards led the pair into a grand room. King Lachlan stood in the corner, looking regal, and a touch impatient.

"You asked to see me?" His smile was strange. It puzzled Talia, but it made the hairs on the back of Chad's neck stand on end.

"Yes, sir." Talia tried to sound brave as she searched the room for the proper spot to display her presentation.

"Leave us," King Lachlan commanded, looking crossly at Chad.

The king's guard promptly left the room, but Chad remained where he stood. "Sir, I would request…" he started, but was brusquely interrupted.

"I said, leave us."

Chad shifted from one foot to the other, then glanced over at Talia, who nodded that she would be okay. He wasn't so convinced, but he also knew he couldn't go against the king's wishes. He excused himself from the room, leaving Talia alone with the king.

King Lachlan advanced towards her, his lips twisted in a half smile. "So, you've come to see what it would be like to be with a king instead of a prince."

"What?" She was taken back. She stepped behind the couch, trying to put as much distance between herself and the king without looking panicked. "Sir, that's not why I'm here."

"But isn't it?" he asked wickedly. He cocked one eyebrow and took another step towards her.

Talia's heart was in her throat as she realized for the first time how different King Lachlan was from his son. "I had a presentation to show you," she offered, inching closer to the wall and eyeing the door that was, by her assessment, much too far away to have any hope of escape. "It's a business arrangement, really."

"Oh, I think there's an arrangement that we can make here today." By now he was advancing on her. He moved to where she stood behind the couch, reaching out his hand to touch her hair. He held a strand of her silky, dark hair in his fingertips, lifting it to his nose to breathe in her scent. "You smell good," he crooned. "It's intoxicating."

Talia closed her eyes to shut out the image of Bryce's father so close to her face. "Please, you can't do this."

"Oh, I can do whatever I want," he announced. "In case you've failed to notice – I. Am. King." He screamed the words at her, and Talia leapt backwards, more frightened than ever.

All at once Chad barged through the door. "I said get out!" the king roared.

"Sir, I would never intentionally be disloyal to you, but I have to stop you from doing something that you'll regret." King Lachlan looked inquisitively at Chad.

"I don't often regret my decisions once my mind is made up."

"Even if it hurts your family?" Chad challenged. And when King Lachlan didn't answer, he continued. "Bryce loves her."

"My son only *thinks* he loves her. He's young. It's an infatuation. This may very well help him get over her." He took another step towards Talia as he spoke.

"It's more than that," Chad argued.

"Chad, no," Talia pleaded once she realized what he was about to reveal.

"I'm sorry," he told her. "Sir," he said, focusing his attention back on the king. "Talia's pregnant with Bryce's child."

A gasp escaped from Talia's lips, but her surprise was nothing compared to the astonished reaction from the king. "That's right," he said. "You're going to be a grandpa. You see, sir, I can't let you do something without knowing all the facts. Hurting her would destroy Bryce, and possibly hurt your own grandbaby."

"Well, this news is something to be celebrated," the king said, smiling, but the smile didn't reach his eyes.

"My actions earlier were only to test your character, surely you know that," the king continued, now looking at Talia. "I was never going to hurt you."

She swallowed and nodded, but without conviction. The king was a terrible liar.

"Chad, why don't you leave us again and let Talia and I get better acquainted. Besides, I believe she has a presentation that she'd like to show me."

Chad looked like he planned to refuse, but Talia nodded in his direction, so he slipped out of the room – waiting outside the door so he could hear her if she called out to him.

"Now, let's see that presentation, shall we?"

Talia was uneasy about the king's demeanor. He was acting cheerful, but something was off. Pretending not to notice, she set up her equipment and began to run through her presentation. She was pleased at how the vibrant colors popped from the holographic images of her charts. The dim lighting of the king's chamber afforded a better visual than her dry run in the bright setting of Bryce's room. As the demonstration continued, her confidence grew.

"You see, sir, this chart demonstrates the types of employment the Comforts could gain if they were free to choose. Many of these ladies are very bright and are passionate about going into nursing, massage therapy, and even teaching. I did have several women who were content with their current, um, profession, so I was thinking an escort service. It would be more reputable, and highly regulated, while still providing an income source."

The king nodded, urging her to continue.

"On this next chart, I've provided a revenue analysis, which includes the total annual income taxes the Comforts would pay if they were in the professions that the job-seeking software paired them with."

The king's eyes glazed over a bit, so Talia picked up the pace, doing her best not to stumble over her words. "As you can see on this graph, I've conducted a cost savings analysis. We can rent out the current housing, either to the existing residents or new tenants, so these cost savings figures include projected rental income. I've partially offset the savings with a year of therapy sessions for each of the Comforts, to help them acclimate to a new way of life, but when you take into account their current cost of care, you can see overall the annual savings is quite significant."

After taking the king through the remaining figures and detailing her strategy, Talia started to feel good about her plan. She'd thought it through and offered solid solutions that would benefit the king financially. He had to be responsive to that, right?

When she was finished, he applauded her, but it seemed forced. "Well, Talia. You've obviously thought this through and have done your research. I think we may be able to accommodate *most* of your proposal."

"Really?" She was shocked.

"I, of course, have one stipulation of my own. It's so inconsequential, it's hardly worth mentioning."

Talia held her breath and waited for the king to reveal his condition.

His expression darkened, and his words turned to poison. "First and foremost, let me tell you a little something about that child you're carrying. That baby will *never* be an accepted part of my family. I'll make sure of that. I'll enact laws to make sure your baby, and no Comfort's baby for that matter, has *any* rights."

Talia's ears burned, and her hands balled into fists at her side.

"And," the king continued, "don't think I didn't notice Kaden's phony sentencing and that patched up confession. I'll bet if I launched an investigation..."

"What's your condition?" she demanded, interrupting his tirade. And with a sinking heart, she listened to King Lachlan's proposal. When all was said and done, she was convinced she'd struck a deal with the devil himself.

Talia fled from the room and into Chad's awaiting arms. "Are you okay?" he asked. "Did he hurt you?"

"No, no," she assured him. "He's just so, so horrible." Deep sobs racked her body. She knew she couldn't reveal the deal that she had just struck with the king, not even to Chad, and it made her feel isolated.

Chad said nothing else. He just held her, stroking her hair as she sobbed into his chest. King Lachlan was right about one thing. Talia was someone to be desired. His profound loyalty to Bryce meant he would never act on or reveal his feelings – but Chad felt deeply for her. More deeply than he'd been willing to admit, even to himself, until this very moment. He seized the opportunity to kiss the top of her head while he patted her silky hair. "Come on, I'll take you back to your room."

When Bryce arrived back home, he noticed that something about Talia seemed off. He quizzed Chad on what she had been up to while he was away, but Chad had sworn to Talia he would not disclose her meeting with the king, so he left that part out of his accounts.

"You know that I love you, right?" Talia asked Bryce that same evening. Bryce observed that she looked dejected. He gathered her in his lap and kissed her, assuring her he'd always be with her – and from somewhere inside she died a thousand deaths because she knew that, unbeknownst to Bryce, forever was not in the cards.

In bed at night, while he lay sleeping, Talia studied his face, although she already knew it by heart. She memorized every inch of him; from the square of his jawline, the faint frown lines that appeared around his blue eyes when he was lost in thought, the small scar on his torso from a bicycle accident as a child, down to the high arches of his feet. Their time together was growing short. She silently prayed she wouldn't forget a thing about him, even though she knew the memory of him would be painful. She caressed her belly, thankful she would always have something to remember him by. She hoped the baby looked just like him.

CHAPTER 28

"ARE YOU GOING to tell me what's wrong?" Bryce asked, his patience wearing thin. Over the past several days Talia had been distant, but today, her demeanor was downright cold.

"I lost the baby," she blurted out before bursting into tears. The tears came easy; not because her words had any ring of truth to them, but because she knew this was the beginning of the end with Bryce. The realization started an ache in her heart she knew she'd never get over.

Bryce looked stricken, and it made Talia feel even worse. She hated hurting him, but she had to think of the bigger picture. This was phase one of the plan. He would never let her leave if he still thought they were going to have a baby. Even if he got over her, he would never let go of his own flesh and blood. *You have to make him believe.* The king's awful words played back in her head. *Your baby will never be an accepted part of this family.*

The prince wanted to ask what happened, and when, but he worried his questions would be misconstrued as blame. Talia was in such a fragile state, he didn't want to lean on her any more than necessary. Heartbroken, he gathered her in his arms and kissed her. "I am so sorry, sweetie. What can I do?"

"There's nothing you can do," she said, realizing the full truth of her statement.

"I'm here for you, *ameerah*, whatever you need."

"Right now, I just need to be alone," she told him, consumed with the guilt of her lies.

He kissed her cheek. "I'll give you some privacy, but I'll be back in a couple of hours. If you need anything while I'm gone, have one of the staff locate me, okay?"

She shrugged, noncommittal.

"Bryce, wait," she called after him. He turned, and walked back to her, leaning down until his face was inches from hers.

"I love you," she told him, unable to help herself. He didn't deserve this pain.

"I love you too, Talia. Everything's going to be okay, I promise."

It was just like Bryce to think he could fix everything. She wondered to herself what his reaction would be if he knew what she was plotting. Hopefully someday he would realize that she had done it all for him, for their baby, and for the good of all the Comforts. *God*, she hoped someday he could forgive her.

When Bryce left the room, he grabbed Chadwick and they headed to *Slim's*, the only bar within the palace walls. The prince never drank in such a public setting, so Chad knew something was wrong. When the pair took their seats on the barstools, the barkeep was momentarily stunned, but quickly recovered. The few patrons scattered around the bar didn't seem to notice.

"What can I get you, sir?" the bartender asked, directing his attention to the prince.

"A pint of the best you have on tap," Chad spoke up, answering for Bryce, "and a club soda for me."

"You got it." The bartender poured the drinks and set them before the two men.

Bryce tossed back the first beer, then ordered another. He drained his second glass before uttering another word. Chad patiently waited on the barstool, nursing his club soda.

"We lost the baby," Bryce finally revealed, not bothering to look up from his now-empty glass.

"What? When?" The news hit Chad hard, twisting his insides. He couldn't bear the thought of Bryce's unhappiness. Or Talia's, if he was being honest.

"I'm not sure. Talia just told me. She said she wanted to be alone."

Chad felt terrible. For both of them. "Well, did she tell you what happened?"

"No."

"Well, did Dr. Thomas confirm that..."

"I don't know," Bryce barked. "She just said she lost it."

Chad grew quiet as he tried to make sense of it all.

"I'm sorry for snapping at you," Bryce said.

"No need to apologize. Just know I'm here for you." Chad returned his attention to his club soda while Bryce worked to compose himself. At a loss for anything constructive to say, the pair remained in companionable silence while the evening stretched on. A melancholy song blared from the speakers, adding to the dismal atmosphere. Bryce pounded down his fifth beer before he announced it was time to turn in.

CHAPTER 29

THREE DAYS AFTER the "loss" of the baby, Talia did her best to patch things up with Bryce. She wasn't sure how long she had with him and didn't want their last days together to be unhappy or strained.

"You seem better today," he told her.

"I feel much better, thank you." She paused and let the guilt surge through her as she thought of the pain she must be causing him. "How have you been?"

"I'm managing," he said. "I just hate to see you like this."

"I'll be okay."

"We can try again," he told her. She offered a wan, noncommittal smile.

"Where do we go from here?" she asked.

"Talia, we're still us. I love you, more than ever. We will get past this and learn to be happy again."

"I'm happy as long as I'm with you," Talia admitted, but sadness marked her delicate features.

Bryce kissed her, and she kissed him back. He wrapped his arms around her and she nuzzled his neck. She knew their time together was coming to an end and she chose to savor every moment.

"I don't suppose we're able to…?" he asked, but she shook her head *no*, not wanting to jeopardize her lie by risking him seeing her bare, ever-growing stomach.

"But we can do other things," she offered seductively, pulling him down on the bed. They fell together in a passionate embrace. For a few stolen moments, they forgot about their troubles, consumed only in each other.

Talia groaned in her sleep, mumbling a small plea Bryce couldn't interpret, but he could tell by the trembling of her lips that she was having a nightmare. Beads of perspiration covered her furrowed brow. He pressed his lips to her forehead, tasted her salty skin, and thought to himself how much he needed her. He'd never wanted anything more, and it perplexed him, the hold she had on him. It pained him to imagine his life without her, and he prayed he'd never have to find out how it would feel.

CHAPTER 30

IT HAD BEEN WEEKS since their encounter, and still nothing from King Lachlan. Talia wondered if he had grown too busy to remember their little arrangement, but she barely dared to hope. She worried about how long she could keep Bryce at bay and how much longer she could hide her growing baby bump. She was now four months along, which was well within the range for finding out with a high degree of accuracy if the baby was a boy or a girl. But she couldn't risk being checked out by any doctors and having Bryce get wind of it.

As she lay in bed, with Bryce snoring softly beside her, she thought about how patient and understanding he'd been since she'd lied and told him she'd lost the baby. He'd cancelled all business trips for the foreseeable future and did his best to be available despite the frequent meetings and appearances on his calendar. When they were alone, she could tell how much he wanted to make love to her, she'd felt the same, but he hadn't pressed the issue. Talia knew she should be relieved, but instead she felt disappointed. She cuddled up closer to him, careful to keep her thick nightgown as a shield between his body and her belly. She reached across him and placed her hand on his chest, her fingers skimming his bare torso.

Bryce stirred, and her heartbeat quickened with excitement. "I need you," she whispered in the dark.

To her pleasure and embarrassment, he whispered back. "It's about time."

Talia sat up in bed and strategically gathered the folds of her nightgown around her middle as she straddled him.

"What's gotten into you?" he said, becoming aroused.

She smiled as his hands fisted in her hair and he pulled her towards him. He kissed her shoulder, her neck, and her chin, before his lips met hers. "Make love to me," she pleaded.

"Gladly," Bryce growled with desire. His hands moved downward and rested on her plump bust area. She sucked in her breath, worried his attentions would drift to her belly and reveal her secret, but her worry proved unwarranted. He remained focused on her ripening breasts. The room was dark, but Talia imagined the puzzled look on his face in response to the obvious changes in her body.

Before Bryce could speculate further, Talia distracted him by taking his arousal into her hands. "Please, make love to me," she repeated, guiding him inside her.

He'd never known Talia to be so bold, and the love and awe he felt for her overpowered him. She tilted her head back as her hips moved up and down in perfect rhythm with his every thrust. His hands once again found her breasts and she smiled at the predictability of it all. Her movements were purposeful and slow – a desperate attempt to make the night last, though she longed for sweet release.

When their lovemaking ended, Talia kissed him again before turning to face the wall. Bryce curved his body around hers and slung one arm over her. "I missed this," he whispered in her ear.

"Me too," she said, and her silent tears hit the pillow as they drifted off to sleep.

Talia was alone in her room, with Bryce booked in solid meetings for the day, when she received word from King Lachlan. A red envelope bearing a watermark of the king's crest was slipped under the door. Within the envelope was a small piece of paper, folded neatly in half.

It's time. Slip past the guard and go to the guest suite, was all it read.

Talia's hands trembled as she hid the envelope and its contents in the folds of her skirt. She knew she needed to think quickly. If she suddenly disappeared, Bryce would come looking for her. She could leave him a note. But she would have to come up with a reason for leaving that would cause him not to come after her – perhaps something that would make him hate her so he'd get over her. Her first thought was to contrive a story about having an affair with Chad. It wouldn't be much of a leap. Bryce had already accused her once, Chad was a good-looking man, and after all, they had been spending so much time together.

She started to write out the note but crumpled it up and threw it into the waste basket. She had to think of a story that wouldn't hurt anyone else; and pretending to have an affair with Chad would destroy a beautiful friendship, not to mention the personal trouble it would cause for Chad. After a few moments of consideration, she crafted a short letter, signed it, and left it open-faced on the bed for Bryce to find when he returned.

Bryce was behind closed doors with a shrewd diplomat when a knock interrupted his meeting. "Come in," he barked. His tone suggested that whomever was interrupting his meeting better have a damn good reason.

"I am so sorry, sir, but it's urgent," his guard told him.

"What is it, Jamison?"

"Well, you see sir, I seem to have lost Talia."

"You what?" Bryce bellowed, rising from his chair. "What do you mean you lost her?" he said more calmly. "She said she was going to stick around the room."

"I know, sir, but she opened the door and told me that she wasn't feeling well and asked that I run to the kitchen and fetch her a glass of club soda. I know I should have had one of the servants do it, but I thought I could be quick and..."

"And what?" Bryce tried hard to keep the panic out of his voice.

"And when I got back to the room, she was gone."

"Okay," Bryce said, exhaling slowly. "I'm sure she just went to one of the shops or something. We probably shouldn't panic." On the outside, he tried to remain controlled, but on the inside, panic was exactly what he was starting to do.

"There's something else," Jamison said, lowering his eyes to the floor in hopes it would swallow him up and he wouldn't have to reveal anything further.

"What?"

"She seems to have left you a note." He held up the note to Bryce, flushing at the knowledge that he had read a large portion of it before realizing what it was.

Bryce took the note but didn't look at it. "Could everyone please excuse me?" Once he stepped out of the room, and out of everyone's line of sight, he finally dared to read it.

Bryce,

I am sorry, but I can no longer stay. I thought I could forgive you for Kaden, but I was wrong. Now that there is no baby, I no longer have a reason to try and make this work. My memories of Kaden are too painful and seeing you every day only makes it worse. Please don't come after me, it'll only cause me more pain.

Talia

The words stung. Bryce crinkled up the note and threw it across the room, missing the waste basket. Part of him always knew he would eventually pay for his role in getting Kaden the job that had caused Talia so much pain, but he had dared to hope that they had moved past that. How could he have been so desperately wrong?

"This meeting is adjourned," Bryce said, returning to the conference room and bowing in respect to the diplomat sitting across from him at the table. "I apologize, but we'll need to reschedule."

He didn't wait for a response before leaving the room again, Jamison in tow. "Find me Chadwick," he ordered.

Bryce had to see it for himself, so he barged into his room, yelling out Talia's name. "Where did you find the note?" he asked.

"On the bed, sir."

Heading to the closet, Bryce, flipped through the racks. "She didn't take anything," he observed, checking the dresser to confirm.

"What's going on?" Chad asked, rushing in.

"Where have you been?" Bryce barked.

"I had the day off, remember? Sasha and I were attempting our first date."

"Oh, sorry." Bryce sounded miserable.

"Never mind about that. What's wrong? Where's Talia?"

"She's gone. She... she left me a note..." His voice trailed off and he took a seat at the foot of the bed.

"Show me the note," Chad demanded, turning to Jamison, who looked perplexed. "The note," he bellowed.

"He threw it away."

"And?"

Jamison slinked away to retrieve the note from the hallway outside the conference room. When he returned, Bryce had his head in his hands and Chad was talking to him in hushed tones. Jamison handed the crinkled note over to Chad.

"Leave us," Chad said after reading the contents of Talia's message. Jamison looked angry at being ordered around by someone he didn't consider his superior, but he nodded and left the room, securing the door behind him.

"You've got to go after her," Chad told Bryce. "This doesn't make any sense."

"No, if I can't give her the space she needs, that proves I'm weak."

"Sir, if I may, it's not weak to care about someone. It makes you human; and that's a quality every good leader should have."

"She made her choice," Bryce said, considering the subject closed. "Now I need to learn to live with it."

CHAPTER 31

TALIA COULDN'T CONTAIN her tears. She cried as she rounded the corner to the guest suite, small suitcase in hand. She'd packed only what would go unnoticed – a single change of clothing, minimal toiletries, and her precious chess piece. She was sobbing by the time the king's personal guard, Kevin, opened the door and ushered her in. But she sat in stony silence as he filled her in on the plans.

"The king secured a house for you outside the city, in one of the neighboring townships. You will be paid a handsome monthly allowance, which will be more than enough for you and your baby to live comfortably."

Talia nodded. "Go on."

"You are not to return to the palace. You are not to reach out to the prince, any member of his family, or anyone under his employ. In exchange, the king agrees to retire the annual Harvest Ball. Each existing Comfort will be given a choice to remain as they are or to find a job of their choosing. Those wanting a different way of life will be given a year of living allowance and will be provided with a therapist and a career counselor to ensure they get back on their feet."

Talia nodded again as another tear escaped her eyes and ran down her cheek. It was the best she could hope for.

"And Bryce?" she asked.

"You mean the prince?" he corrected.

"How will I know that he's okay?"

"Well, that's not really your concern, now is it?" he sneered.

Kevin led Talia down a corridor and into a wing of the castle she'd never seen. When they arrived outside of a doorway, she gave him a questioning look. Ignoring her, he pressed his palm to a small screen mounted to the right of the door. The screen scanned his hand, then Talia heard the door unlock. The guard opened the door and stepped inside, motioning Talia through before closing the door behind them. The door automatically locked once they were inside.

The room was small, and furniture was sparse. A wing-backed chair, end table, and tall corner lamp were all the small space had to offer. On the far end of the room was a gas fireplace. The thick coat of dust on the glass indicated it hadn't been used in some time. The fireplace was surrounded by a built-in bookcase. The bookcase held few books, and the volumes it did hold were dusty and unnoteworthy.

Kevin crossed the room to the bookshelf. His fingers fumbled along the lip of the bottom shelf until he found a hidden button, which he pressed, then stepped back as the bookshelf swung open and away from the wall – revealing a hidden door. Talia stared at the door, wide-eyed.

"Let's go," he barked, snatching the suitcase from her hand. He slipped through the door and Talia followed close behind.

The door closed automatically behind them and she heard the bookshelf reengage with a thud. In front of them was a long, dimly lit corridor. Talia's imagination began to work overtime. Where he taking her? What if this was a trap and she was being led to a secret dungeon?

"Where are you taking me?" she demanded.

"To your new home," the guard snapped, not bothering to look at her. He walked ahead, his long legs moving in quick strides, and Talia found it difficult to keep up.

"Can you slow down?"

Kevin stopped, crossing his arms in annoyance. "Quit stalling."

"Please," she said, gazing up at him through red-rimmed eyes. He huffed in disapproval and continued down the hall, but he slowed his pace.

The corridor sloped downward. The incline was steep, and after some time Talia realized that they were underground. "Is this a secret, underground tunnel that leads out of the city?" She was awestruck, momentarily forgetting her plight.

"The tunnel is used to allow the king and his royal guard passage in and out of the palace walls without being noticed." Kevin spoke the words *royal guard* with a puffed chest.

Talia nodded in fascination. Besides her few trips with Bryce, she hadn't been outside the palace walls for two years. A lump formed in her throat as a wave of nostalgia hit her. Perhaps she could find where her childhood home had once stood. She smiled to herself at the thought.

After some time, the floor began to slope upwards. "We're getting close," Kevin said. When they reached the end of the corridor there were steps leading up to a hatch. The guard entered a code on the panel near the top of the stairs and the hatch swung open. Talia expected bright sunlight, but instead she found herself in another small room. This room was cheery and cluttered with furniture. The self-closing hatch disappeared into the overwhelming design of the faux-tiled floor.

"Where are we?" she asked.

"At a safe-house just outside of the palace," Kevin told her. "There's a car waiting for us outside." His tone had softened, and Talia wondered if he felt guilt for what he was doing to her.

Talia stared out the window in disinterest throughout most of the car ride. The car passed through several aging neighborhoods with overgrown yards, faded paint, and sagging rooflines. She perked up when the road widened, and the homes became further spaced apart. By her estimation, the yards in this neighborhood were at least half an acre. When the driver came to a stop in front of a one-story gray house with cream trim, an arched wooden door, and generous front porch, she smiled for the first time that day.

"For me?" she asked, her voice hopeful.

"This will be your home."

Talia stepped out of the car. The weight on her chest lessoned at the thought of raising her baby in a safe place away from the king, in a house that was all hers. She never imagined a middle-class neighborhood still existed and the prospect of the people finding their way out of poverty beyond the palace walls gave her hope. "It's pretty," she said aloud. A flagstone, tulip-lined pathway led up to the front porch. A wooden porch swing swayed in the breeze and Talia fought the urge to try it out.

Kevin joined her on the porch, set her suitcase on the stoop, and fished around in his pockets. He pulled out a single key and handed it to her. "For you," he said.

Talia closed her hand around the key and pulled it close to her chest. Her hands trembled in anticipation as she fiddled with the lock. She swung the door wide open and stared inside. The house was light and airy with an open concept, despite its small size. She loved it at once.

"Go in," Kevin said, startling Talia who had forgotten he was standing there.

She entered the house and the lights came on automatically. "The home has several modern features," Kevin told her. "I think you'll find it rather comfortable."

The thought of never hearing Bryce's voice echoing through the house filled her with loneliness, but she forced a brave smile. "It's beautiful," she said.

"The house comes fully furnished, but you are welcome to redecorate any way you wish. Your living allowance should be enough for you to do so. In the sitting room, you'll find a computer. You can do much of your shopping online if you choose, but there is a small town just a few miles up the road.

"I jotted down your banking information," Kevin continued, pulling a scrap of paper from his shirt pocket. "The first six months' living allowance has already been placed in your account." He handed her the piece of paper, which she took, embarrassed. She hated charity, but she would swallow her pride for the sake of her baby.

"Thank you," was all she could manage to say.

Kevin nodded. "Well, I'll leave you then. Remember, you are not to contact any…"

"I remember the deal," Talia spat out.

"Very well then." And with that, Kevin dismissed himself from her presence, leaving her alone with her tortured thoughts.

When Kevin left, Talia wanted to throw herself on the sofa and have a good cry, but she didn't want her first memories alone in the house to be filled with sorrow. Instead, she squared her shoulders and wandered to the kitchen. Despite the small size, the kitchen was designed to make the most of the space. There was a beautiful island, with two bar stools, and the appliances included a double-oven and an industrial-sized fridge. The cupboard space was modest, but adequate.

Talia opened each cupboard, pleased to find new dishware, a toaster, and other such amenities. Beyond the kitchen was a breakfast nook with a bay window that offered a view of her expansive side-yard. The master bedroom was on the far corner of the house. She was pleased to find a queen-sized bed and a solid, mahogany dresser. The walk-in closet held several gowns and shoes. The clothing was not as glamorous as she'd become accustomed to, but it was well-made and would suit her needs. Amongst the gowns were maternity dresses for the coming months.

At seeing all the effort that went into her new home, and that she would want for nothing, Talia wondered if the king had a softer side than she had thought, or if every detail was a reminder of the bargain she'd struck and a warning not to go back on her word. She shrugged off the last thought and continued with the tour of her new home.

Next to the master was another bedroom that Talia supposed would be the baby's room. The door was closed, and she held her breath for what she would see inside. Although she was grateful for the furnishings, she didn't think she could bear to have her baby sleep in anything that a member of the king's staff had chosen.

When she swung the door open and peered inside, she breathed a sigh of relief. The room was a decent size. A dark, wooden rocking chair was perched in the corner, next to the window. Other than the chair and the white, sheer curtains that adorned the window and gave the room an airy feeling, the room was empty. Talia made a mental note to order a crib and changing table to complete the room and smiled at the thought of being able to pick it out herself.

The remainder of the house held another bathroom, a laundry room with a door that led to a one-car garage, and a sitting room lined with windows that Talia decided would make a perfect room for reading. She wandered through the house once more, taking it all in. Afterwards, tour complete, and emotions running high, she finally allowed herself to crawl into a ball in her new bed and have herself a good cry.

CHAPTER 32

"HAVE A PLEASANT morning, Talia," a computer-generated voice prompted as Talia entered *Sam's General Store* for the second time that week.

At hearing her name, the store owner looked up from behind the counter. "Good morning, Talia," he greeted her warmly.

"Good morning, Sam," she said, offering her brightest smile. Most days smiling took significant effort, but with Sam it came easy.

"What's your fancy today, love?" he asked, stroking his salt-and-pepper beard.

"I'm looking for a small cut of prime rib and fresh apricots."

"Got a cravin' again, eh?"

Talia blushed. "It seems so, yes."

"Your little one is lucky to have such a good mum already looking after its needs." Sam cast her a wink and Talia blushed again at the compliment. "I'll call back to the butcher and let him know you're headed that way," he offered.

Talia thanked him and headed toward the back. Sam had been good to her since her first visit to his store. He was kind without asking too many probing questions and was the closest thing to a friend that she had these days. He was like a doting grandfather – at least what she imagined a doting grandfather would be like.

Armed with a cut of meat, a carton of milk, and a bag of apricots, Talia made her way back to the checkout counter. Her heart caught in her throat when she glanced up at the television screen. A female reporter in a dreadful orange gown stood in the palace courtyard, just outside the housing for the virgin Comforts.

"Sam, can you turn that up?" Talia set her items on the counter, eyes glued to the screen.

"The city had mixed emotions after today's announcement that the palace will not be sending out scouts to recruit the next crop of Comforts." The reporter paused for impact, but her timing was all wrong.

"While there has not yet been an official statement from the king, one of the palace's most trusted informants has confirmed that recruiters were told to stand down. Many speculate the decision was made in response to recent protests and the growing demands for equality. We're being told that the funds typically used for the annual recruiting process will be diverted to a charity of the king's choosing. There has been no word as to whether or not the next annual Harvest Ball will be cancelled and what will become of the Comforts already awaiting their opportunity."

"Opportunity," Sam snarled in disgust, muting the T.V. "Should I put this on your account?" he asked, directing his attention back to Talia.

Talia felt dazed. She shook her head *no* and handed over cash. She wanted to throttle the reporter for her poor choice of words, but the reality of the news story was setting in. King Lachlan was starting to honor his side of the bargain. She felt dizzy and the floor swayed beneath her. Sam ran around to the front of the counter and took her by the arm.

"You okay, kiddo?" he asked. "Carl, grab Talia some water, will 'ya?" he called to the butcher in the back.

Sam helped her to a chair behind the counter and she sat down without argument. Her hands shook as she accepted the water Carl offered her. "I'm sorry," she apologized after taking a sip. "It must be the pregnancy."

The store owner gave her an inquisitive look but didn't challenge her. "Just take a moment," he told her.

"Do you want to talk about it?" Sam asked once he'd given Talia a few minutes to recover.

She started to decline, but instead blurted out, "I used to be a Comfort." She avoided eye contact, feeling the shame of her admission.

Sam patted her hand as she shared her story, at least the parts she felt she could without betraying any confidences. "I'm sorry to unload all of this on you," she said, finally through with spilling her guts to the kind old man who was a stranger a few short weeks earlier.

"Listen here and listen good," he told her, taking on a firm demeanor. "You are lovely, and you are brave. You and your baby are going to sail through this just fine."

Talia smiled, grateful for the vote of confidence.

"But if there's anything you need along the way, I'm happy to oblige," he offered, patting her hand once more.

"I appreciate that, Sam," she told him. "But you're right, my baby and I are going to be fine." She stood to her feet and squared her shoulders.

"Thatta girl." He kissed her cheek and offered her a hanky. "Now get that cut of meat home before it spoils."

CHAPTER 33

"I JUST DON'T GET IT," Bryce admitted aloud to Chad for the hundredth time in recent weeks. He tossed back a shot of whiskey and slammed the glass down on the coffee table. He was brooding and looking to Chad for answers – the only person in the world he would allow to see him in such poor shape. During the day he put on a brave face for his subjects, but the dark circles under his eyes and less-than-cheerful demeanor hinted that he wasn't his usual self.

Chad stood by, helpless, wrestling with his own conscience as he witnessed Bryce's unraveling. He knew he should tell Bryce about Talia's meeting with the king, but he worried about how the news would be received. He knew it had been wrong to keep the meeting a secret from Bryce, but the consequences of that secret were far greater than he could have imagined. He'd let his feelings for Talia cloud his judgement.

"Out with it, Chad," Bryce commanded, as if reading his mind.

Chad took a deep breath. "Talia had a private meeting with your father a few weeks before she left."

"She what!" Bryce leapt out of his chair and started to pace. "How could you let this happen?" he accused, throwing his hands in the air. "Don't you know what kind of man my father is?"

"Talia assured me that nothing happened. At least nothing like you're thinking."

"And you believed her?"

"Have you ever known her to lie?" Chad asked, casting a pointed glance at Bryce.

"No, I suppose not." Bryce returned to his seat.

"I know your father wouldn't have touched her," Chad began, although he decided to leave out the little part about revealing Talia's pregnancy. "But something else happened in that room. Talia was so upset when she left, and she never seemed the same afterwards."

Bryce leaned over in his chair and rested his head in his hands. "If he touched her, I'll kill him."

"Careful," Chad warned. His eyes darted around the room, worried they would be overheard.

"I am completely serious. In fact, I'm going to talk to him right now."

Moments later Bryce arrived outside his father's living quarters. The king's guard positioned himself in front of the door, denying entry. "I'm going in to see him, Kevin," Bryce announced.

"I'm sorry sir, but I've been ordered not to allow any visitors."

"I said, I'm going in to see him."

Kevin widened his stance and refused to budge. "Dad! Dad! You'd better open this damn door," Bryce hollered.

The door flew open, but it was Bryce's mother who answered instead. "Shh, keep your voice down," she scolded.

"I need to speak with him alone, Mom," he told her, softening his voice for her benefit.

"I'm afraid that won't be possible." Bryce started to argue but stopped himself when he noticed the pained look on his mother's face. She opened the door wider and motioned him in, securing the door behind them. In the far corner of the room Bryce saw his father lying in bed, tubes hooked up all around him. His father's personal physician hovered over the bed, checking vitals and tinkering with the machines that lined the king's bedside.

"What happened?" Bryce asked.

"It happened a few hours ago," Grace explained. "He seems to have had some sort of stroke. The doctor is doing everything he can, but..." Her voice trailed off as she choked back tears.

"Why didn't anyone tell me?" he whispered. He was still angry with his father, but it was his mother he worried about. She was a strong woman, but Bryce knew how she cherished his father and wondered how she'd get along without him if it came to that.

"At first, I thought he'd snap out of this." Grace waved her hand in the direction of the bed. "But I also couldn't worry about word getting out. The kingdom will be in a panic if there is uncertainty about who is in charge. There's already been so much political unrest..."

Bryce felt a twinge of guilt at her last remark, knowing he was largely responsible for much of the unrest. "What is your prognosis?" he demanded, turning his attention to the physician.

The doctor shook his head. "I'm not sure. He might wake up from this. Then again, he might not." The doctor glanced over at Grace and mouthed an apology for his candor.

"On a positive note, the instrument on the left here measures brain activity, and so far what I am seeing is very positive."

"So, what does that mean?" the queen demanded.

"I'm afraid it means we'll just have to wait and see."

After ensuring that his mother would be fine by herself, Bryce trudged back to his room. Chad stood outside the door, faithful as always. He resisted the urge to ask Bryce what had happened but felt certain the prince would confide in him anyways. He was wrong. Wordlessly, Bryce entered his room, then dismissed Chad for the evening, telling him that he was going to turn in early.

CHAPTER 34

TALIA SMILED to herself as she strolled along the gravel road, grocery bags in hand. Over the past several weeks she'd fallen into a comfortable routine of walking the couple of miles to town to buy groceries at *Sam's General Store* and to pick up fresh bread from the bakery. There was still a large hole in her heart. She missed Bryce desperately. But the joy of feeling his baby grow inside her and the knowledge that she would have the means to raise their baby on her own were great sources of comfort. She was also enjoying her newfound freedom, coming and going as she pleased.

Using her living allowance, Talia had ordered the crib and bedding for her baby. She found a new doctor in town who was willing to make house calls. Dr. Jessing was an older, female doctor who was both pleasant and thorough. Talia took an instant liking to her. The doctor confirmed that everything with the pregnancy was progressing as normal, but Talia asked that she not reveal the sex of the baby. She didn't feel right about finding out that sort of news without Bryce. It would feel like a betrayal. She did ponder baby names. She had decided on Grace if it was a girl; and Gabriel if it was a boy – after her father.

Despite her contentment with her new living arrangements, and her commitment to choose happiness, Talia cried herself to sleep most nights. She never imagined she'd need Bryce so badly. It pained her to be without him. As much as she'd like to blame the side-effects of her pregnancy for her flood of tears, she knew the despair she felt went beyond changing hormones.

On her long walks, Talia considered what she would do once the king fulfilled his promise and the Comforts were freed. She thought perhaps she would reach out to them; find out how they were fairing. Seeing them happy might curb her loneliness and remind her of why she made the sacrifice. Perhaps she'd ask Sephora or Rachel if they'd like to move in with her. The house wasn't big, but she supposed she and her baby could share a room. So far, she hadn't heard of any Comforts being freed, but the news that there wouldn't be any new recruits was promising. She'd also heard rumblings in town that the annual Harvest Ball was going to be cancelled. She prayed the rumors were true and that it was another sign of the king making good on his promises.

Talia was misty-eyed as she caressed her stomach. "Everything's going to work out for the best," she whispered to her unborn child. A tear rolled down her cheek as she spoke, and she let it fall to the earth.

CHAPTER 35

THE KING'S PASSING came as a shock to everyone – most of all his attending physician. Once the king regained consciousness and was able to recall his name and carry on a private conversation with his wife, the doctor was confident of a full recovery. But then the king took a turn for the worst, slipped into a coma, and never woke up.

Grace delivered the news to her son in person. She remained calm, regal. "I will have the council prepare the ceremony. Tomorrow we will make the announcement, and immediately after you will be sworn in and crowned king."

"Mom, you don't have to arrange all of this yourself," Bryce told her.

She offered him a bright smile. "No, I'd like to. It'll keep me busy. Plus, the less people that know about this until then, the better. I think your father would be proud to…" And just like that, her cheerful facade crumbled, and she began to weep.

Bryce put his arms around her and pulled her in for a close hug. His mother had never been much of a hugger, so he thought the hug would feel awkward, but it didn't. Grace sobbed for several moments as he patted her back. He couldn't bring himself to cry with her. He had too many suspicions about his father; suspicions that had spilled over into hatred over the past several days.

"Let's move," Bryce said to both Jamison and Chad, stepping into the hallway once his mother was gone and he had taken a few moments to get his emotions under control. His jaw was set in a hard line and both men knew better than to ask where they were going.

The prince moved through the palace hallways at a brisk pace, his guards in tow. It took a few moments for Chad to realize where they were headed. He'd escorted Bryce through this maze of corridors on many occasions over the past several months, mostly under the cover of night. They entered the secret tunnel through the hidden room and ended up on the outskirts of the palace where a delivery truck awaited them. Jamison looked perplexed, but he remained silent. The delivery door on the passenger side of the truck slid open and the three men slipped inside.

When they arrived at the safe house, Bryce motioned for his guards to follow him inside. The invitation surprised Chad, who had been directed to stay outside and keep watch on previous visits. The house was jampacked with men and women wearing white armbands with an embroidered Royal Bluebell flower.

"These are the protestors," Jamison observed.

Bryce nodded, then turned to address the crowd of people huddled in the living room. "First, I wanted to say, 'thank you' for all of your help over the past several months. With your countless hours of effort, you've helped build awareness for my campaign. The kingdom is demanding a change, and I owe that to all of you." Jamison's jaw nearly hit the floor, but Chad wore a look of pride.

Pausing to take a breath, Bryce squared his shoulders. His tone was somber when he continued. "There will be an announcement in the morning that you will all be interested in. I can't tell you what it is, but I will tell you that it means our plans will be accelerated. In the weeks to come, you will see a sweeping, yet peaceful change." Bryce emphasized *peaceful* as he spoke. "I am counting on each of you to help keep everyone engaged, but *calm*."

The room exploded into applause, and Bryce nodded modestly.

"I didn't tell you about all of that because I wanted to protect you from having to lie for me," Bryce explained to Jamison once they were back at Bryce's chambers. "It wasn't because I didn't trust you."

"Well, it appeared Chadwick knew what was going on," Jamison sulked.

Chad grunted as if it made no difference to him either way. But inside he glowed. The trust the prince had in him was of the upmost importance. He knew he'd almost lost that trust and was relieved at Bryce's forgiveness when Chad finally came clean about Talia's meeting with the late king.

"Chad has been a close friend and confidant for many years," Bryce explained. "It is my hope that you and I are reaching that same place."

After sensing some hesitation, he said, "Unless I'm wrong." He kept his eyes trained on Jamison's.

"No, you're not wrong," the guard replied, still smarting from not being included sooner but glad to be part of the close bond he'd always envied between Chad and the prince.

When morning came, the gates of the kingdom were opened to the townspeople with a promise of a crucial proclamation. Thousands gathered in the streets in anticipation, unaware they were about to witness Bryce being crowned king. The council and founding families agreed that allowing the people to watch the ceremony would increase acceptance of their new leader. The council issued the official announcement of the king's passing, followed by a brief yet moving speech from Bryce. His eyes scanned the crowd during his speech, hoping to catch a glimpse of Talia amongst the onlookers. If she was out there, he didn't see her.

When Bryce was crowned, there was a thunderous applause from his subjects, followed by dancing and singing in the streets. Grace stood by his side as he waved to the crowd. The people of Inizi had renewed hope. The new king stood tall, confident, but inside he prayed their hope wasn't misplaced.

"You know what this means, right?" his mother asked softly once the crowds dispersed and she and Bryce had a private moment.

"Yes Mom, I'm aware." He tried to keep the edge out of his voice but dreaded the inevitable. Now that he'd been made king, he had within the month to choose his queen.

Following the ceremony, Bryce and the council worked late into the night. As new king, his first order of business was to bring on additional members of the council. More change was coming, but for the time-being he needed a couple men he could trust while he implemented the actions requiring immediate attention. If the old members of the council disagreed with his approach, they didn't let on. New laws were drafted and posted. At the end of an exhausting day, Bryce was proud of what had been accomplished, though there was still much work to be done.

The funeral was held the following day. Despite the late king's declining popularity, the walls of the kingdom were lined with flowers, balloons, letters, and candles. Shops were closed, and throngs of mourners took to the streets, following alongside the funeral procession. Amongst the mourners were patrons holding signs announcing their respect and appreciation for the new king.

The convoy of black sedans passed through the gates of the kingdom and drove the short distance to the family cemetery. A wreath of white roses was fastened to the bonnet of each car. Only members of the royal family, the guard, and the five founding families were allowed at the graveside. The onlookers remained a respectful distance beyond the boundaries of the graveyard.

Bryce held his mother's hand as the priest offered comforting words about a great man who had a love for his people and whose home was now in a better place. The compassionate man the priest described was not a man Bryce had ever met. He closed his eyes and tried to imagine such a man once existed somewhere inside his late father. As the coffin was lowered into the earth, he heard the haunting sound of the crowd singing Amazing Grace.

After the funeral, Bryce escorted his mother back to her room while Kevin and another guard trailed close behind. Bryce wrapped Grace in a bear hug once they were within the privacy of her room. "I have something else to tell you," she said, her face buried in his shirt. "It's something that your father revealed before he died."

She felt her son stiffen and she knew he feared the worst. "He never touched Talia," she said quickly, pulling back to look at him. "It's important that you know that. But there was something else." She began to reveal the deal King Lachlan made with Talia; the deal that drove her away, perhaps for good.

Bryce's head was spinning. "I have to sit down," he said, doing his best to process everything. *So perhaps Talia still loved him. Maybe there was still a chance for them.* "Wait… wait you're saying Dad *knew* that Talia was pregnant?"

"Yes. He told her that she had to find a way to make you believe that…" Grace stopped mid-sentence, as if she too was just realizing the magnitude of what King Lachlan had confessed.

"That means Talia didn't really lose the baby," Bryce said. "He told her to lie." He knew that he should feel deep hatred for his father, but instead all he felt was relief. And hope.

Grace hung her head. "I'm sorry Bryce, I had no idea."

"Oh Mom, you couldn't have known," he assured her. "I never trusted him, and I didn't even suspect such a thing." He pulled his mother in for another hug. "Dad was always lucky to have someone like you." It

225

was the best he could do. The new king didn't have any kind words to offer in remembrance of his father.

News traveled fast in a small kingdom. When Talia received word that the king had passed, she felt a conflicting sense of relief and despair. Her first instinct was to reach out to Bryce, but she wasn't certain that he would want to hear from her. By now he must hate her for leaving him. Not to mention he never came after her when she left. Perhaps he didn't love her like she thought he did.

If that were the case, she wouldn't want to tie him down with an unwanted commitment. She knew that even if Bryce's feelings had changed, he would still want to stay with her out of some misguided chivalry and that was the last thing she wanted for her or her baby – to be someone's undesired obligation.

Talia's hand moved to her belly and she caressed the bump that was forming. She was thankful that she would have something to remember Bryce by. This life that grew inside her was what would get her through this heartbreak. Maybe after some time passed she would reach out to Grace. It was only fair that the queen be aware that she had a grandbaby. Then again, what if Grace demanded that Bryce *do the right thing*? Talia was torn on what to do, so she pushed her tormented thoughts aside and made herself busy tidying up the small house the late king purchased for her in return for her silence.

226

CHAPTER 36

"WHERE DID YOU TAKE HER?" the former queen demanded of Kevin.

"To whom are you referring to?" the guard asked, pretending to be mystified.

Although she knew she should admire his loyalty to her late husband, Grace grew more impatient. "I know," she told him flatly. "The king confessed everything before he died. Now I want to know where you carted Talia off to."

"My Queen, I don't…" Kevin stammered. He was stalling.

"She is carrying my unborn grandchild," Grace said, raising her voice. "You will tell me now."

Kevin turned white, then about three shades of purple. "My Queen, I swore to your husband that…"

"Where, Kevin?" she demanded. Her tone was brusque, and she offered no words of forgiveness or understanding. Defeated and ashamed, Kevin hung his head and revealed all that he knew.

Talia shot upwards from where she had been napping on the couch, believing she heard a knock at her front door. But who could be visiting her? She waited in silence until she heard it again. This time it sounded more urgent. Rising from the couch, Talia smoothed her skirts and scurried to the door, opening it cautiously.

Bryce stood before her, dressed casually in jeans and a ball cap. At seeing his stern expression, Talia took two steps backwards. When he moved towards her, Talia squeezed her eyes shut, putting a protective hand over her growing belly.

"Talia, I'm not going to…" Bryce started.

"I know," Talia said, letting out a deep breath and counting backwards from three slowly in her head before she felt confident enough to open her eyes and face him. "I would deserve it though," she said meekly.

Bryce stepped past her and into the living room, motioning his guards to remain on the front stoop. He closed the door so he and Talia could be completely alone. "May I?" he asked, stretching out his hand and looking down at Talia's protruding stomach.

She nodded in response and watched in silent awe as he knelt in front of her. She fought the urge to run her fingers through his dark hair. He'd let it grow out more since she'd last seen him. He'd tried to tame it under the ball cap, but dark locks of hair poked out the brim and grazed his neckline. Bryce placed his hand on her belly, then leaned in, planting a kiss just below her navel. "Your mamma gave me quite a scare," he said, talking at Talia's midsection. He stood to his feet, looking pointedly at her.

Her face turned crimson and she burst into tears. "Bryce, I'm so sorry. Please let me explain. The day that I left…"

"None of that is important now," he told her, cutting her off. He didn't want to relive that painful day. He hated to see Talia cry, and he ached to hold her and tell her it was all going to be alright. But now that he was king, he had more than his desires to consider.

"We have much to discuss, but now isn't the time." The tenderness from moments earlier had vanished.

"Bryce, can't we…"

He interrupted her. "Pack what you need. I'll send someone back to get the rest of your things."

Talia nodded. She grabbed a suitcase from the hall closet and headed to her bedroom, shoulders slumped. Bryce didn't follow her. He waited by the doorway, face set in stone.

She emerged moments later, clutching the chess piece he'd given her. "There's nothing else here that I need," she said.

Bryce couldn't agree more, but he kept the sentiment to himself. He needed to be strong. "Let's go," he barked.

When they reached the front porch, Talia spotted Chad amongst the guards waiting outside. She wanted to run to him, to lean on him like she'd done so many times, but she knew the awkward position she'd already put him in and vowed not to put him through that again.

"You're going to ride with Chadwick," Bryce said. "I'll follow in the car behind you."

Sensing that she wasn't in a position to argue, Talia nodded and allowed Chad to escort her to the car. She was stunned by Bryce's cold indifference. She slipped into the backseat, Chad sliding in beside her. As the car pulled out of the drive, both were silent. It was Chad who finally broke the awkward silence.

"Talia, I was wrong to set up that meeting with the king. To go behind Bryce's back. I know that now. I had to make it right with Bryce and repair some trust that was lost."

"I am so sorry Chad. I never should have asked you to do that."

"I was happy to do anything for you," he admitted. "That was part of the problem. I struggled to balance my feelings for you and my loyalty to Bryce. I failed."

Talia flung her arms around his neck and kissed his cheek. "You are a cherished friend," she told him. But instead of returning the hug, Chad disentangled himself and took her hands in his, keeping her at arm's length.

"I got too close," he told her. "It can't happen again. It won't happen again." He kept his eyes trained on hers.

She nodded and returned her hands to her lap. She thought she understood. During the course of their friendship, she'd shared confidences with Chad that he'd upheld. Even from Bryce. Chad now felt like he'd betrayed his friend by doing so. She hadn't thought of it as a betrayal at the time.

But Chad knew she didn't fully understand. She couldn't possibly – and he could never tell her; never let her know his true feelings. His heart constricted. He swallowed the sweet agony that seeing her again brought him; pushed it down deep. He knew it was going to be his pain to endure;

knew he would see her and protect her every day, but she would never be his. He also knew he would eventually get over it. Sasha was helping him with that. He'd been honest with Sasha about his feelings from the start.

"Where are we going?" Talia asked, breaking the silence once more.

"There's something Bryce wanted me to show you."

Her heart flip-flopped. Maybe she'd misread Bryce's reaction to their reunion. Her interest was piqued. "What is it?"

"You'll see." Chad winked at her, and Talia was glad to see traces of his lighthearted self.

When their convoy arrived at the palace gates, the car went straight instead of taking a right towards the palace. To Talia's disappointment, the car Bryce rode in turned right.

"Bryce won't be joining us?" She couldn't hide the disappointment in her voice.

Chad looked equally confused. "He probably wanted you to see it without any distractions," he offered.

The car drove to the far end of the palace grounds. What used to be empty fields was now a bustling construction site of new homes. Saw blades shrieked and workers scurried about. The car stopped in front of the construction site and Talia got out. The air was thick with sawdust and the smell of sheetrock.

"What is all this?" she asked.

Chad smiled. "You're looking at the new neighborhood of affordable housing for the Comforts. Actually, we don't call them Comforts anymore."

"They've all been freed?" She hugged Chad in her excitement but this time he didn't pull away.

"Well, the ones that wanted to be, yes," he explained. "Sadly, there are several that wished to stay put. Baby steps."

Talia felt a pang of sadness, but not enough to cloud her joy. "Will one of these homes be for Sasha?"

Chad smiled. "That one right there," he pointed to one of the framed buildings.

"What about Sephora?"

Chad stroked his chin in thought. "May I see those plans?" he asked a passerby foreman, who obliged.

They walked through the maze of construction as Chad pointed out who would occupy each house. "That one in the corner will be Sephora's. Madelyn's will be beside hers. Then Rachel's."

Talia thought her heart might burst with happiness for her friends. "And Bryce arranged all this? In such a short time?"

"Most of it was already being planned," Chad admitted. "He just didn't know how soon he'd have an opportunity to implement his plans."

She stared at the mass of structures, taking it all in. "He really is amazing," she said. "He's going to be a great king."

Chad couldn't agree more.

Back in the car, Chad turned to face her. "I am glad you're back."

Talia grinned in his direction. "Me too. Is it still okay if I call you Chad?"

"Of course. Talia, we're still friends. You just have to know that anything you share with me will be shared with Bryce."

She nodded. "Chad, I will never put you in that position again. And you should know that if Bryce gives me another chance, I will never keep anything from him."

"Another chance?" he was confused. He'd assumed she and Bryce had worked everything out back at her house.

A single tear slid down her cheek, which she quickly extinguished. She was already slipping back into old habits. "Poor choice of words," she said, smiling through her tears. "I'm sure it will be fine."

Chad took her hand in his and allowed himself to pretend one last time that what they had was more than a friendship. He knew it was the last time he would touch her this way and he savored the moment.

When the car arrived at the palace, he gave her hand one last squeeze. "It's going to be okay," he promised.

Talia wasn't so sure, and she let out a labored breath. She wanted to give him another hug, but she feared it might be crossing a line. "Thank you," she said instead. "You will always be a friend."

The words cut Chad deeper than she would ever know. He helped her out of the car. "Lady Grace would like a meeting with you first," he told her.

She was anxious to see Bryce but allowed Chad to lead her to Grace's suite – the suite Grace once shared with the late king. Her heart hammered in her chest. She felt ill thinking of the last time she'd visited this room.

"Chad, I don't think I can face Kevin again," she admitted before they'd reached the doorway.

"Kevin has been relieved of his duties."

Relief washed over her. When they reached the door, a young man with kind eyes and thinning hair greeted them.

"Good afternoon Chad. And you must be Talia," the young man said, reaching out to shake her hand.

Talia shook his hand and felt instantly at ease. "Yes, it's nice to meet you. And you are?"

"I'm Dillon, the new guard," he said proudly. "I'm very pleased to meet you. The queen, err, Lady Grace, is expecting you."

Talia took a deep breath. She wasn't sure what to expect. But when she saw Grace, all anxiety evaporated. Both ladies embraced like old friends. Chad and Dillon bowed politely, then closed the door to offer the women some privacy.

"It is so great to see you," Talia told her.

"That is kind of you to say. I was worried you wouldn't want to see me after what my hus..." Grace's words caught in her throat and a sob escaped her lips.

Talia pulled her into a fierce hug. "No matter what happened, I would never blame you. I consider you a true friend. And please believe me when I say how truly sorry I am for your loss."

Grace smiled and dabbed at her eyes. "My late husband confessed everything before he passed. I know I was blind to many of his faults, but I never imagined..." She paused, collecting herself. "I would have done whatever I could to protect you, had I known," she explained. "And I know my son would have too."

Talia felt a twinge of guilt. She couldn't bring herself to ask how much Bryce knew. She figured it was her place to explain to him.

"I should have opened up. To both of you," Talia said. "And I never should have lied about losing the baby."

Grace patted her hand. "I understand why you did it. A mother will do anything to protect her baby. Even if it means giving up the man she loves."

A tear slipped past Talia's lid and streaked down her face. "I just hope Bryce will forgive me."

"He would be a fool not to," Grace said. "No matter what happens, I will always consider you my daughter."

CHAPTER 37

WHEN CHAD ESCORTED Talia to Bryce's door and left her standing outside it, her mind drifted back to the day not so long ago when she'd met Bryce for the first time. So much had changed since that day, but she felt just as terrified; once again not knowing what to expect. If Bryce had already made up his mind that it was over between them, Talia wondered why he was dragging it out.

Her hand shook as she reached up to knock on the door. She longed for the days when his bedchambers were also considered hers. Where did everything go so wrong?

Bryce opened the door and stepped aside to let her in. He closed the door after them and locked it. She couldn't recall the last time he'd done that. It left her unnerved.

As before, Talia tried to appear brave as she pushed her way into the room, but this time she took a seat on the edge of the bed. Bryce sat beside her. He didn't touch her.

236

"I was sorry to hear about your father," she said after several moments passed. "I know you weren't very close, but he was still your father."

The new king grunted in response.

Talia had a feeling he was dismissing her, but she wasn't going to let him go without a fight. She stood to face him.

"Bryce, I'm sorry," she said miserably. Her shoulders shook as she stammered through her explanation. "Your father and I made a deal. I'd tell you I lost the baby and go away, he'd release the Comforts and step down, letting you take the throne. He told me that he would never let our baby be a part of his family. He also said he'd never step down from power or release any of the Comforts unless I left." By now she was sobbing.

"My note," she continued. "Bryce, I didn't mean any of it. I don't think like that."

Bryce couldn't keep up his stony facade any longer. "Talia, it's okay," he said. His tone softened as he stood to look at her. He drew her close to him and wrapped her in his arms. He wanted to hold her and never let go.

"Talia, I already know," he whispered. "My mother told me everything. My father confided in her before he died." He pulled back from her, studying her. "I just wish you would have told me." He stroked her tearstained cheek with his thumb. "You should have told me," he said more firmly.

"That was part of the agreement. He said the deal was off if I told you. I thought it was the only way."

He took both of her hands in his and kissed her knuckles. "You are very brave, and it amazes me how strong you are. But *ameerah*, I had everything under control."

"What do you mean?" she sniffed. Her heart fluttered with renewed hope of his forgiveness.

"Talia, why do you think I've been away on business so much? Much of my business hasn't been too far past the palace walls. I have been trying to gain support for an administration more self-governing in nature; drafting laws that would free the Comforts and give them a fair shot in society. I've also been traveling to the Grand Americas to learn more about their government and to work with their top advisors."

Bryce continued to talk in great depth about his plans to force his father into retirement and to establish a governmental advisory board once his father stepped down and he was king. The advisory board would be a voice for the people and would have the power to keep the monarchy in check. He was working to develop plans that would help the poor – programs that would create jobs and royal decrees forbidding the wealthy landlords from imposing hefty taxes on their tenants. Talia learned Bryce was even responsible for organizing the protestors, trying to mount awareness and support amongst the people in preparation for his future campaign.

"You see, before I could invoke change, the people had to be ready for a change. They had to demand it. If I attempted a sweeping change without the support of the people, both within and outside the walls of the palace, there'd be danger of a violent revolt. I couldn't put my people or my family in that kind of jeopardy." He cupped her chin. "I couldn't take that risk with you."

"That's quite an elaborate plan." She took a step back to gaze up at him. "And to think, I just presented your father with some holographic pie charts," she muttered.

"What?" Bryce couldn't help but chuckle.

"You know. Pie charts. Statistics about the type of employment the Comforts could be offered if they were freed, how the taxes they paid on their wages would benefit the kingdom's economy, stuff like that."

"And you did all of the research yourself?"

"Well, Chad helped some, and I conducted a lot of interviews with the Comforts to gather ideas."

Bryce's smile vanished. "That's the other thing we need to discuss." His tone was grave once more. "Chad."

Talia nodded as fear and anxiety crept down her spine. "Did Chad get in any sort of trouble for arranging the meeting I had with your father?"

Bryce was silent for a moment. "I understand that he did it for you."

"That's not really an answer," she pressed gently.

"No," he sighed. "No, he didn't. But we are going to need to establish boundaries. Chad is our friend, but he is also my lead guard and I need to know that he is always honest with me. Our safety depends on it. And I need to know that you are always honest with me," he said pointedly. "Or none of this is going to work."

Talia was silent as she considered his words. She knew they weren't intended as a threat. Bryce was speaking the truth.

"Chad and I already spoke," she said. "I'm assuming that's why you wanted us to ride together?"

Bryce nodded. "And?"

"And we agreed that we would never keep any secrets from you. But I also let Chad know that I would never put him in that position again. I will always be honest with you Bryce, always."

"That's what I needed to hear," he said. "I love you Talia, but as king I have bigger responsibilities now. I need to make sure the people I surround myself with are trustworthy; that we have mutual candor and understanding."

She was silent, letting his words sink in.

"I agree," she said after some time. And she knew if she wanted to secure his forgiveness, she should probably leave it at that. But he'd asked her for the truth, and if she was going to be honest, she had much more to say. "But the keyword is *mutual*," she continued. "I also need you to be honest with me. Not leave me in the dark."

Bryce paused to consider her point.

"I love that you want to protect me," she told him. "I love that you want to protect our baby. But you can't expect me to sit in this room day after day and wait for you to come home to me. I want to be out there doing something. I want to be by your side – sharing ideas, implementing change. It should be a partnership." Her tears were flowing once more, and she didn't bother to hold them back. "I am willing to do anything if you'll take me back, and if that means being holed up in this room every day, I'll do it. But you should know that it might come at a cost. I don't want to resent that you managed to free every Comfort but one."

Talia's shoulders shook with anger. She hadn't realized how much she'd been holding inside.

Bryce was dazed. He'd only meant to protect her. He hadn't realized in doing so he'd kept her caged. He took her in his arms and held her tight. He felt sorrow and relief all at once. Relief they were both willing to talk through their issues, but sadness that he'd been so blind to his own actions and how they impacted the woman he loved. He never wanted to snuff out the fire she possessed, the fire that had drawn him to her. Bryce kissed her softly, brushing away her tears.

"I think we've both learned a valuable lesson here," he admitted, easing away to study her. "Perhaps we could have been spared some pain if we'd been more honest with each other."

Talia nodded in agreement. "I am so sorry," she told him again. "I never wanted to leave. I was just naïve enough to think I was helping things."

"It's okay, *ameerah*. I know why you did it. God, I was so angry when you left, but I get it now. I should have been more open with you about my plans. I just didn't want to get your hopes up."

"And you're not angry with me anymore?" Her heart thudded in her chest as she searched his face for the forgiveness she desperately needed.

He breathed a deep sigh. "I'm not angry," he assured her. "I just needed to be sure where we stood with each other."

"I promise to always be honest with you, Bryce," she told him again. "But you should know I wouldn't change anything if it was the only way to bring us back together."

"And Talia, I promise I will never keep you in the dark again. And I will never make you feel confined. It was never my intention."

"I know."

"And in the spirit of full disclosure, you should know I have one last secret I've been holding back because I wanted to surprise you."

"What's that?" she asked, wiping her eyes with the back of her hand.

He smiled. "Just got signed this morning. It's a new law that allows Comforts to marry whomever they please, even noblemen." He paused, looking sheepish. "Even royalty." And before Talia had time to realize what was happening, Bryce was down on one knee and fishing a small box out of his shirt pocket.

"What are you doing?" she asked, her eyes shimmering with excitement.

"Talia Delaney. Will you do me the honor of being my wife?" Bryce held Talia's gaze as he waited for an answer.

She stared down in shock at the ring. It was a beautiful arrangement of diamonds wrapped around a large, princess-cut sapphire – elegant and tasteful.

"Yes, of course I will marry you!" Eyes filled with tears, she allowed him to slip the ring on her finger. He stood to his feet and she slid her arms around his middle.

"I love you," she whispered. "I was so sure you were done loving me."

"*Ameerah*, I've only gotten started," Bryce whispered back. He buried his face in her hair, drinking her in. "Pie charts," he murmured in her ear, chuckling to himself.

"Hey, they were some pretty fancy, and well thought-out, pie charts," she laughed.

"I don't doubt that." He cupped her chin in his hand and gazed down at her. "I really do love everything about you." He needed her to know. It was important to him that she felt secure and loved after everything she'd been through. After everything he'd put her through.

A smile played across her lips and he could tell she believed him. He wrapped his arms around her waist and pulled her close. "I'm never letting you go, Talia."

"I won't let you," she told him.

When Bryce announced that Talia would be his queen, his approval ratings climbed. To those less fortunate, the queen-to-be was living proof that anyone could change their fate. Little girls named their dollies *Talia* and performed make-believe weddings in the streets. Sometimes they convinced the little boys to play along – recruiting them for the part of parson. Or groom.

To the wealthy families of Inizi, she embodied beauty and grace – qualities they held in high esteem. Bryce held his breath for the backlash surrounding Talia's upbringing, and was prepared to protect her fiercely from it, but there was very little negative publicity. Any that materialized was quickly squashed.

The wedding was a stunning affair. Talia wanted to keep it small, intimate, but Bryce's advisors suggested that opening the ceremony up to as many guests as possible would further increase popularity with the new king and queen. It was a point neither Bryce nor Talia could argue. The palace cathedral was small, so the wedding was to be held outdoors – a decision that made the wedding coordinators nervous, but the weather cooperated.

The wedding coordinators commissioned DeMarco, a famous fashion designer from the Grand Americas, to oversee the attire for the new king and his queen-to-be. DeMarco's vision was to slingshot Inizi's fashion into the latest century, while maintaining a touch of the old-style. Bryce was outfitted in a modern fit, black tuxedo, complete with a silver bowtie and matching cummerbund. Bryce was a good sport but drew the line at the designer's suggestion of a cane and top hat.

A white satin wedding dress with chiffon overlay was specifically designed with Talia's pregnancy in mind. With the empire waist and flowing veil, DeMarco did his best to hide Talia's growing midsection, a feat he reasonably succeeded at.

The ceremony was held in the main courtyard with the castle as a backdrop and the impressive marble fountain as a focal point. The palace grounds were a sea of lush greenery, mixed florals, and white, well-lit tents. And people. Thousands of people. Extra chairs were brought in, but multitudes of onlookers lined the streets both within and outside the gates.

The orchestra played the bridal march as Talia made her way down the grassy aisle to where Bryce awaited. She felt a wave of sadness in remembrance of her parents. Their passing meant her father couldn't be present to give her away and that she wouldn't catch a glimpse of her mother watching teary-eyed from the audience. But Talia's newfound happiness overshadowed the immense loss.

She held an impressive bouquet of white roses with a subtle sprinkling of Royal Bluebells. Most onlookers assumed she was keeping with the tradition of *something blue*. But to the protestors who believed in Bryce even before he was king, and helped him raise awareness for his cause, the flowers meant so much more. They symbolized patronage. And hope.

Bryce thought Talia glowed as she walked towards him. She seemed to float across the aisle of grass and white tulip petals. When she reached him, his blue eyes locked with hers, the woman he loved with his whole heart. His bride was as lovely as ever as she stood before him, barefoot and shrouded in white.

"And now the couple will exchange the vows they wrote for each other," the priest announced. The fountain babbled irreverently, but the crowd fell silent as the couple recited the vows. The words came easily. Honesty. Truth. Respect. Partnership.

Amongst the guests were several Comforts, though they'd successfully blended with society and were no longer referred to as such. Sephora, Rachel, and Sasha were all in attendance and lined the second row Talia reserved specifically for her friends. The blushing bride was proud to see that Chad accompanied Sasha to the wedding, having been given the night off. Rachel brought a date Talia didn't recognize. Sephora sat alone, graceful and beautiful as always.

Talia worried someone in the audience might object to the union – her beginnings being humble and somewhat scandalous, not to mention her pregnant state. She had considered asking the priest to remove that portion of the ritual but thought better of it.

Her fears were unwarranted. No one objected. When the final vows were spoken, and the couple kissed and were presented as king and queen, the crowd cheered. Music could be heard in the streets, far beyond the ceremony. Floating paper lanterns filled the sky.

The baby was announced in the weeks following the wedding. It was to be a boy. The couple planned to name him Gabriel, after Talia's late father. There were gifts, well-wishes, and only minor rumblings from some of the more old-fashioned subjects. Grace made the announcement herself – gushing at the prospect of becoming a grandmother.

CHAPTER 38

TALIA SQUIRMED in her seat, wringing her hands. She concentrated on the hair pins that lined the vanity and silently reminded herself to *remain calm*.

"Your hair is going to look lopsided if you keep moving," Rebecca scolded.

"I'm sorry, I'm just so nervous."

Bryce entered the room and walked up behind the two women. "You ready for your speech, my queen?"

Although her back was to him, Talia caught his eye in the reflection of the mirror and made a face at him. She was getting used to the term, but still preferred *ameerah*. "Ugh, I hope so. I don't know that I'll be any good at public speaking."

"You will do great," he told her. "Just remember that everybody loves you. And don't forget to breathe."

Rebecca sprayed Talia's hair and gave it one last pat before announcing she was finished. Talia gazed at her reflection and smiled. "It looks really nice, Rebecca. Thank you."

The former handmaid smiled back, curtsied, then after casting a nervous glance in Bryce's direction, scurried from the room. Despite how kind Bryce treated Rebecca, and how hard he tried, he still made her nervous. The memories of how the late king, Bryce's father, had treated her were still fresh.

Once Rebecca left the room, Bryce asked, "Will she ever like me?" He feigned offense, but he was chuckling.

Talia glanced up at him. "Probably not. But hey, she made me look fantastic." She smoothed her hair and shot him a playful wink.

He leaned down, kissed her cheek, then helped her to her feet. Moving around was proving more difficult the closer she got to her due date. "You look adorable," Bryce told her.

They walked out together to greet the people. Talia placed one hand in his and the other on her abdomen. Chad followed close behind, Sasha's hand pressed firmly in his. It made Talia's heart soar to see the two of them so happy. Chad had been standoffish the first few months after her return, and she was relieved to see him look so happy and carefree.

When she stepped up to the microphone, the new queen felt a wave of self-doubt. But the enthusiastic cheers from the crowd grounded her. Reminded her of her purpose. "Good morning," she started.

"Good morning," the crowd echoed back in unison.

"Thank you for coming out today. I'm going to pretend that you're all here for me, and not the delicious pastries Frances prepared for afterwards."

There was laughter and a few whoops of agreement from the people.

Once the noise settled, Talia continued. "I'd liked to talk to you about positive change, and the part each of us plays…"

Bryce watched with fondness as his new queen delivered the speech she'd prepared. Despite her small stature, she stood big and bold. Her presence was both benevolent and commanding – a perfect balance. How much she'd changed him. How much she'd change his people. Their people. He thought of how he'd kept her so protected in the beginning. In doing so, he'd almost lost her. He now recognized the strength she wielded. Everyone needed protection; but now he and Talia protected each other. They were a united front. And soon they would have a little one to protect. Together.

After Talia finished her speech, and the thunderous applause died down, Bryce took her by the hand once more. He was more in awe of her than ever. "Are you aware how much I love you?" he whispered.

"Yes, you tell me every day," she laughed. "But are you aware that although I love you, right now you're the only thing standing between me and one of Frances' pastries?"

"Well, at least we know where we stand with each other," he laughed.

"Yes, we do," she agreed. "Side by side. Unless you're too slow to the food line. Now let's go eat."

Acknowledgements

As always, I would like to thank my family and friends for their overwhelming support. Thank you to the brave souls, my book club included, who came along on the journey – reading early versions of the novel and offering both encouragement and feedback. Your kindness will not be forgotten.

To my husband and two daughters, you deserve the most praise. Thank you for your understanding as I pursue my writing dream. I know the time to write and promote cuts into precious family time and I greatly appreciate your sacrifice. And to you, the reader – thank you. Thank you for taking a chance on a new author and for being a part of my make-believe world. I hope you enjoyed the voyage.

About the Author

Blake Channels was born in Tri-Cities, Washington where she resides today with her husband and two children. She graduated from Washington State University and is a wife, mother, and office professional by day and a writer in her heart and soul – and whenever her busy schedule allows. In addition to writing romance novels, Blake enjoys spending time with family and friends, camping, and curling up with a good book.

Made in the USA
Columbia, SC
10 May 2023

16369610R00157